THE FALL OF PARTHA

STEVE STEPHENSON
K.M. TEDRICK

Black Rose Writing | Texas

ISBN: 978-1-68433-903-7
PUBLISHED BY BLACK ROSE WRITING
www.blackrosewriting.com

Printed in the United States of America
Suggested Retail Price (SRP) $19.95

The Fall of Partha is printed in Book Antiqua

*As a planet-friendly publisher, Black Rose Writing does its best to eliminate unnecessary waste to reduce paper usage and energy costs, while never compromising the reading experience. As a result, the final word count vs. page count may not meet common expectations.

Cover Art by J. Caleb Designs
Editing by Robert Carr

THE FALL OF PARTHA

CHAPTER ONE

A n evil goddess named Adois had coveted the world of Muiria ever since her twin brother had sown the seeds of life on that barren piece of rock.

Her brother, Adaman, had created the Staff of Adaman to protect the planet, and he had searched the world until he found a man wise in the ways of sorcery and he entrusted him with the staff.

Adaman was pleased that dragons had decided to come through the void to settle on this newly habitable planet, Muiria. They created a source for good on the budding paradise, and pleased with his creation, he forbade his evil twin sister from ever interfering with that world.

Adois then became even more jealous of her brother and his new "toy," as she called it. She waited eons, until the world was populated, before she felt ready to act. She placed a whisper here, an item there, and felt that soon the precious Muiria would fall into her own evil hands.

Adois knew that only a person of good allegiance could hold her brother's Staff of Adaman and that anyone would have to study the staff itself before creating a copy for her own. She sought out a man of pure heart to retrieve the staff of Adaman and make a replica. That man would have to be tricked into taking the staff.

Soon her innocent thief realized what Adois wanted to accomplish and he tried to use the staff against the goddess, but he wasn't strong enough to defeat her, even with its magic staff. In one last defiant act, he separated the crystal from the mythril staff and thereby rendered it impotent.

While doing so, though, he had allowed the goddess to handle the pieces of the staff and they provided Adois with more than enough information than she needed to create her own staff. She vainly called hers the Staff of Adois, since her brother had named his the same way.

Adois now needed someone from Muiria with pure evil in his heart to make her an alternate copy of her brother's staff which she could adorn with her own magic crystal. She easily enchanted a warlock to do her bidding and brought him into the misty realm in which she dwelt.

Adois called forth the fire elementals and the forging of her staff began. She poured all her malice through the warlock himself into the creation of the staff. The fire elementals hammered a shaft so strong that the mightiest blade would not be able to shatter it and at one end of the new Staff of Adois, her minion mounted a dark gem that Adois had infused with all of her dark arts.

When it was finished, she was delighted.

The warlock she had used was left a mere husk of himself after the strenuous forging and he died on the forge's floor. Her brother's staff would have no defense against this one because his had been taken apart and no longer had its crystal.

Adois' ultimate plan was for the two staffs to be drawn together to shroud the world in darkness. She had to wait countless eons for the loss of the Staff of Adaman to bring about the desired effect on Muiria and envelop the planet in an initial shroud of darkness until finally she discovered one who might serve her well.

She knew her brother had created a staff of light to keep the darkness at bay, but her staff would bring all the darkness needed to encompass Muiria so she could take that world over from her brother. She hid the piece she had of the Staff of Adaman within her own domain.

Discovering what had occurred, Adaman secretly went to Adois' realm and sought the remnant of his own staff. He flew down towards the dark planet that his sister called home, but when he entered her realm, he found it crowded with demons from the nine hells. It was a world the exact opposite of Muiria and evil radiated from the barren rock it was made of.

As he began the search for his staff, Adaman could feel the power that he had infused into the artifact and he honed in on its hiding place. His sister had not yet detected his presence.

He landed outside of a dark cave and, calling forth a white light, he descended into the depths of the hole. The chamber was crowded with demons to protect the staff, but the white light he produced repelled the beasts and they melted back into secret hiding places. After hours of enduring the rank odor that the demons had left behind, Adaman came upon the original staff of his own making. It lay upon a smooth rock and three demon lords guarded it.

The white light had no effect on these creatures and so he drew his sword. They dueled for many turns of the clock, clashing swords and casting spells. The battle was long and soon Adaman was covered in the green ichor that was the blood of these demon lords. Adaman's spells left great wounds on the foul beasts while he received deep slashes from them. The creature's weapons cut deep into the god's body, but as fast as they injured Adaman, he quickly healed.

The battle continued in the white-lit stones of the cave. Soon the god prevailed and the demon lords were vanquished in a battle more vicious than any Adaman had had in eons.

He picked up his own staff then and began his flight out of the cave system. The lesser demons he met along the way were destroyed by the light that now emanated from his staff alone.

Once out of the cave the staff was drawn to its crystal and it pulled Adaman with it towards the gem. The staff soon reached a speed that only a god could withstand and in the matter of half a turn of the clock he was approaching his sister's castle through a darkness that blended into the inkiness of his sister's world.

His sister was away from her castle and Adaman had the dark place to himself, but her guards were not demons. They were men deformed by the evil of the world on which they lived, and his staff could not incinerate them.

As Adaman advanced, he had to fight off hundreds of the deformities, but their non- magical weapons merely bounced off the skin of the god. His own sword sang as he swung it and killed dozens of the evil warriors and threw their dead bodies high into the air. He made his way deeper into the castle toward the pure crystal calling to him and the deformed warriors disappeared.

Adaman entered a huge cavern and in the middle was the crystal, floating in midair. As he approached it, he began to feel the wards that his sister had placed around the treasure to protect it. Time after time the wards attacked Adaman, but his godly powers kept him from being injured. Soon the crystal was within his reach.

Then he heard a screech behind him. Adois stood there, her staff raised to strike.

Adaman took a blow to the back of his shoulder. The pain was immense. A second strike drove him into a kneeling position before he was able to strike back with his staff. His power of good outweighed the power of evil which Adois had poured into her staff and she was thrown across the room. Adaman reached up and grasped his crystal and smiled at his sister before he blinked from her view and returned magically back to his own realm.

Adois slumped to the floor and cried out in rage.

Adaman thought, correctly, that his sister would assume that he'd hide the staff back in his own native realm. Instead he took the crystal and the staff back to Muiria and entrusted them to the wood elves for safe keeping.

Their immortal race hid the pieces in their most sacred and guarded place and locked it away in a chest of pure alabaster.

Adois knew that now was the time to strike, before the Staff of Adaman could be fully re-assembled by her brother. She picked out one man in particular for this task, an able and, more importantly, a cruel, evil man. Zachary the First, the Emperor of Zeiglon, was to be her puppet in this endeavor. He would grasp for power like a newborn calf for its mother's milk and Adois knew she could manipulate this power hungry and malicious man beyond any other ordinary denizen on the planet of Muiria.

On a black night, heavy with rain clouds and booming thunder, with jagged flashes of lighting, she came to the evil being's quarters in the Zeiglon capital.

Zachary lay snoring in his four-poster bed and seeing him, Adois had second thoughts. Was this truly the man she wanted to entrust her staff to?

Adois was wearing her most revealing silk dress and she took her own staff and slammed it down on the smooth marble floor, shattering it like the glass. Zachary awoke with a shudder.

"What's the meaning of this? Guards!"

"My dear Emperor, sound cannot escape this chamber," Adois said. "I have made it so. I have come to offer you riches beyond your wildest dreams. Do not be afraid."

Fully awake, the Emperor sat up in bed. "What do you mean by riches beyond my wildest dreams? I myself can dream of the vastest of fortunes."

She continued, "I have created a magical staff that will lead you to victory over your foes and provide you with ultimate power over this world." She knew she had set the hook. Men are so easily to manipulate, she thought.

His greed and his aching for the ultimate power surged through him, but Zachary looked at her, still questioning.

"Why offer me such a gift and not someone else?"

"I have watched you for a long time, Zachary. Long ago you forsook my brother and became my follower. That, I applaud. By using the power infused in my staff, you can now become the most powerful man on Muiria. Need I say more?"

She tossed the staff to him and he deftly caught it.

He could feel the evil power pulsing through it and instantly he envisioned himself being crowned Emperor of the World.

"How does it work, my lady?" he asked.

"That you must discover on your own. But rest assured, you will find out sooner rather than later. It will have dominion over lesser men and its jewel is enhanced by my own magic."

He could feel the staff bonding with him. Suddenly a greedy, most evil realization entered his mind.

He pointed it at Adois. He thought of fire. A huge gush of flame traveled across the floor and appeared to engulf the goddess.

As it cleared, he saw that the fire had not touched her. Instead, it had stopped a few paces in front of her and she had formed a shield against any further attacks against her. She was unhurt.

Before he could draw another breath, she was beside him her, left hand wrapped around his throat, and she lifted him out of his bed and pushed his head against the wall.

"Do not *ever* presume to use the staff against me again! Above all else, this staff is mine. Its first allegiance will always be to me, and it will never harm me. Do you understand?" she asked and she gave his body a vicious shake.

She released him and Zachary choked and gasped for breath before slumping down onto the bed, coughing.

"Yes…goddess, please," he managed to gasp.

"Now, my Emperor, here is what I want you to do. My brother, curse his name, created another such staff. I have ferreted out that the staff is held by the wood elves until such a day as evil threatens the peace of this world."

She watched him carefully and saw not fear, but resolve creep into his eyes.

"You must use my staff," she said, "to obtain the Staff of Adaman."

"Yes," he said a little too eagerly.

"It will not be so easily taken," Adois warned. "Only one of good nature can use the item so you will be incapable yourself of using the pieces or joining them together. Only a person born of goodness may reassemble it."

She eyed him to make sure he understood her point, without question. He did.

"Now, my staff can open a hole through the void, that dark nothingness between the planets, creating a passage where you can emerge where my brother's staff is kept," she instructed. "Once there, your minions can take the staff, but remember, only a person of goodness can place the jewel back on the head of the staff. Never assemble Adaman's staff yourself or touch the staffs together in the same place. The power they would unleash would be immense and would be destructive to the entire world...including you. Keep the pieces of my brother's staff as trinkets. Lock them away, throw them into the sea. I care not. But it will be safer for all if they are held in secret by the one holding my staff."

The emperor regarded her in silence, but intently.

"Heed my advice, Zachary," Adois said. "What I have given, I can take away with a mere thought, and it will leave you a shivering, drooling shadow of your former self."

With that final warning she walked seductively away from him and disappeared. Zachary rose from his bed, wide-awake and fondled the magical staff that the goddess had just given him. Images of ruling the world were foremost in his thoughts.

Chapter Two

Celedant was fishing off one of Dragon Isle's natural jetties and smiling as he enjoyed the warm sunshine and gently breezes. He noticed he was being approached by a silent man wearing the garb of a guardsman and holding a missive.

Celedant opened the letter he was given with shaking hands and he smiled broadly. He would normally have been considered too young for the magical academy to choose him, but he read in the acceptance letter that he was to report to Edain, where potential wizards and sorceresses were taught.

He gathered his fishing gear and began the long hike home.

Celedant had been born in the Dragon Isles to a sorceress mother and one of the captains of the guard. They were wonderful and caring parents, and his mother was proud that her son was gifted enough to follow in her footsteps, but she cried when she heard he was accepted into the academy.

He left to live the austere life of a young wizard. He had grown up with his parents on the southernmost section of the island chain, and it was the first time that he would be living away from home. It was also his first visit Edain, the center of the magical world. All he knew of the place was that the city protected the Dragon's Tear, a talisman that had been built at the beginning of time by the first dragons to arrive on the planet from the void. The Dragon Tear acted as a beacon to other dragons and kept the order of good and evil in check on the world of Muiria.

After arriving at the docks in Edain, Celedant met his mentor and advisor Capres, a white-haired wizard of undeterminable age. He would prove to be a stern teacher, but a jolly man…when he wanted to be. Celedant had taken to the old man instantly.

After five years of diligent study with Capres and others, Celedant had become quite a child prodigy, and this pleased his friend and advisor beyond telling. The Masters of Dragon Isle had encouraged their friendship because they knew that Celedant would one day venture forth as a full wizard and a second set of eyes was needed to keep watch on the young man and steer him in the right direction and accustom him to the ways of the outside world.

One day Celedant, his long, straight brown hair gathered in a ponytail, recognized he himself had become restless. He felt he had accomplished all there was to at Edain, and he wanted to explore the greater world. He and his best friend Azimuth, the dragon, had begun to dream together of the adventures that awaited them in the outside world.

The young wizard Celedant showed great promise, and it was determined that his youthful dragon, Azimuth, could gain much experience if he traveled with the wizard.

There was one deeply kept secret to most of the world. Dragons had the ability to transform into elves and wolves. The elves were the only other immortals in the world, and a transformed dragon could then pass among the population without being detected. This led to the common misconception that there were no true dragons on Muiria and people therefore thought that fire drakes were actually dragons. The dragons found that idea disgusting, but they tolerated the fallacy to keep the secret of their elven existence intact. Celedant and Azimuth were bound to keep this secret if they went out into the world.

In Celedant's sixth year it was time for his bonding with Azimuth. After each wizard and sorceress had passed their fifth year at the academy, they were bonded to a dragon and that bond would last the lifetime of the dragon and its partner. There was never any doubt as to which dragon would bond with the Celedant. Azimuth and he had grown up together on the isle roaming the grounds of the castle and nicking fresh pies from the kitchen as youngsters. Azimuth, a golden dragon, was the eldest son of Bendaryl, a silver dragon and the king of the dragons. His mate and queen, Saradyntl, was a stunning dragon with emerald green with jewel-like scales.

The bonding ceremony was to take place on the northernmost isle, where the main dragon aerie was located. Saradyntl and Capres would oversee the ceremony. For their flight to the aerie Celedant and Capres mounted a great silver dragon and were followed in the air by the other master wizards. Celedant's family rode on his mother's green dragon.

All the dragons landed on the great outcropping of stone which marked the main entrance to the aerie's caves. Once they had all landed and their riders had dismounted, Azimuth joined Celedant in a procession. The masters went first, accompanied by their bonded dragons, and were followed by the young Azimuth and Celedant.

They entered the main aerie, where hundreds of dragons perched on ledges to watch the procession, and the dragon queen joined them and led them upward on a winding passage massive enough for the dragons to travel on. Before long, they all reached the cave's opening on the side of the mountain, overlooking the sea. Celedant and Azimuth were escorted up an incline to a flat ledge and were made to stand side by side while the masters began an incantation. Shortly the Queen dragon began her own conjuration.

A reddish light coalesced between the dragon queen's front claws and with a shove she sent a glowing light flying to encompass Celedant and Azimuth. She then began moving her claws in a delicate fashion and weaving the energy surrounding Celedant and Azimuth. Small threads of energy were pulled from one of them and bound to the other, not unlike weaving a fabric, and the lighted strands glowed brighter as the woven aura became more complex.

Finally the two of them stood facing the Queen and the glowing threads linked them like a spider web.

"Thus, by these threads, you are bound for life," the Queen said.

She clapped her great claws together and the bright light that had surrounded Azimuth and Celedant vanished. They both fell toward the ground.

If it had not been for the quick reactions of Capres and his silver dragon, they would have crashed to the stone, but they were caught before impact.

Celedant awoke in his dark cell in the south wing of the castle. Somewhat disoriented, he knew that he must have been transported back there by the masters. He felt a slight tingle in his mind and suddenly, as if from a great distance, he felt he heard Azimuth and he registered the dragon's telepathy at once.

Azimuth do you hear me? he called mentally.

Yes, I do, the dragon answered. *This is part of the binding that I have heard about, but it is so different to experience it now firsthand.*

Yes, Celedant thought back to him. *I have read of it too, but this is quite astonishing. You actually sound as if you're in a well.*

It will get more powerful as we age. Celedant, can you see all my thoughts? Azimuth asked.

No, only those you project, Celedant replied.

Your head will clear and you'll come to new understanding, I think. I am told it is more difficult for a wizard and a sorceress than it is between the dragons.

In the next few weeks Azimuth and Celedant worked on their skills in telepathy as they rested by the seaside. The dragon also developed his ability to transform into his elven shape. His attempts were slow at first and more often than not he came out as a very odd-looking elf. But as he continued to practice, he began transforming into a perfect elf with ease. He did not have to practice transforming into a wolf more than a couple times because a wolf's body was so much simpler than that of an elf.

Soon the two were conversing with ease and Azimuth had begun to learn how to make his elven form speak. It was difficult at first, but he used his considerable intellect and magical spells to help him become fluent in the common tongue of humans and elves, and in another similar language of the Iles.

Azimuth was still too gangly a youth for Celedant to ride upon yet, but that did not stop them from trying. The times they did, one or the other ended up casting a levitation spell to block the other's fall.

Soon Azimuth learned to breathe fire, too. In his first feeble attempt, a small cloud of smoke puffed out. The first time that happened, a small round puff came out, sounding almost like a burp, and Celedant broke out in laughter and rolled on the ground in mirth. Azimuth gave him a cross look and shot out another small flame, also with a burp, and it landed on the ground right next to his friend. That brought the wizard to his feet, and now it was time for the dragon to roll on the ground in mirth. Seeing the humor in it himself, Celedant let out a bark of laughter and joined his friend in their merriment.

Once Azimuth had mastered this new skill, bright flames erupted from his maw and heated the air for some distance in front of him.

Nearly twelve years passed since their first bonding and Celedant was deemed ready to venture forth on his own, with Azimuth as his companion. The dragon had now grown enough for Celedant to ride him, and Azimuth's flaming skills were superb.

CHAPTER THREE

Zachary assembled the men he would send to retrieve the staff of Adaman. He had selected the best, most trusted of his warriors, along with one warlock of considerable power, to attempt to steal the staff. The emperor dressed the men in plain clothing and armor so the elves could not trace them to Zachary himself as the perpetrator of the theft. He had no idea what his men were to expect as they went to procure the prize, but the men were well chosen, and he had no doubt they would succeed.

He called them to gather around him and gave them the information they needed to accomplish his task.

"You will be transported to a treasure vault in the wood elves' capital, Ravannhiel. You are to ignore the other treasures there and seek out only two objects, the crystal and the accompanying staff. You are looking for an alabaster box. It should be about six or seven paces long. In it is your prize. Any questions?"

Even if they had a question for the emperor, they were too frightened of their master to ask.

Zachary grasped the staff of Adois and prayed to the goddess to aid him in opening the rift to the Staff of Adaman. Words formed in his head, and he began. The staff tight in his hand, he repeated the words the goddess had implanted in his mind and watched in amazement as a dark rift—which they often called the void—opened through time and space.

On the other side of the rift, in the capital city of the wood elves, his men saw a trellis covered with green flowering plants intertwined with the wood, which gently swayed on a huge tree branch.

The soldiers took a step into the void and out onto the massive causeway leading across the dark rift. One of the soldiers tripped as he entered. He waved his arms to try and catch himself, but his momentum carried him downward to drift into the black nothingness of the void. He would die from the fall or be eaten by the denizens who called the void their home.

The remaining soldiers stepped off the causeway and onto a huge tree limb. There was an instant shout of alarm as they materialized out of thin air in front of two elven guards. The sword play between them was short-lived.

The elves had halberds that were unwieldy against men with swords in such close-range combat. Using the shaft of his weapon to block the swords, one guard drove the wicked tip of his weapon through one of the trespassing humans. He loosened his grip on the halberd and drew his own sword to engage the next intruder. The first elven guard was down, and the lone elf found himself facing a man who was better at sword play. He never had a chance. His attacker struck out with his boot and kicked the elf outward into the depths of the forest.

Zachary's marauders quickly tossed the remaining elf after him, followed by the dead body of their own fallen warrior.

The door that the elves had been protecting stood shining in the moonlight, its surface perfectly cut from the trunk of the tree. One man knelt at the keyhole and went to work trying to pick the lock. Suddenly an elven arrow pierced one of the intruders, knocking him from the tree. As the others returned fire, the man at the lock heard a click, opened the doors, and stepped back for the warlock with them to enter.

Beyond was a treasure room, but the warlock did not fixate on the piles of gold and delicate objects around him. He was looking for one thing. With a simple location spell, he soon found the alabaster box that held the pieces of the Staff of Adaman.

As the warlock retrieved it, he heard the sound of swords clashing against swords on the tree branch behind him. He hurried back out and found his soldiers engaged in a severe fight with a group of elven guards. He watched as the man next to him pitched off the walkway to the forest floor, an elven arrow sticking through his eye.

More elven arrows then began picking off the thieves with ease.

Two others were engaged in combat near the opening to the void and the warlock called to them. The remaining interlopers disappeared within the rift and it closed as soon as the last man entered.

The elves were confused and alarmed as to what had happened and were unsure what had been taken. After a thorough search, they were horrified to discover the loss of Adaman's Staff and realized that those men had come through the void to steal it. The elves knew of the void from their ancient texts and the knowledge gleaned from the dragons, but they had never considered the thought that someone might actually use it to enter their realm, let alone to make off with the precious staff.

The thieves returned to Zeiglon and Zachary the Emperor closed the gate behind them. Less than half of his band had returned safely. He ordered two men to deposit the heavy alabaster box on a small table next to his throne and then he dismissed them.

Zachary ran a hand over the delicately carved container and admired the elven workmanship. He opened the box and saw the two pieces of the Staff of Adaman wrapped in silk and tucked inside. He lifted up the staff and the jewel and could feel the power emanating from the separate pieces.

CHAPTER FOUR

Zeiglon and its neighbor to the north, Partha had been at odds for centuries.

In a new attempt to ease border tensions, the Parthians had asked the elves to send an emissary of theirs to Zeiglon in hopes of securing an agreement of peace. Aedith, the Wood Elf King's son, headed the diplomatic venture.

Such expeditions were known to always end in failure, but the elves were optimistic that they could gain some sort of truce this time. The elven delegation consisted of the prince and five advisors as well as fifty of the king's famed elven guards, dressed in chain mail with dark green cloaks.

The Zeiglon king readily acquiesced to the elves request for a peaceful meeting, welcoming the chance himself to sort through a centuries' old struggle. That time frame was merely a passing moment to the immortal elves, of course, but it had remained a bitter continuous struggle for the short-lived men.

When the party reached the gated entrance of Zeiglon, the Sergeant of the Guard stopped and bade them wait until the king's advisor could be summoned. The advisor, Victor, kept them waiting outside the gates for nearly a turn of the clock before finally showing up. If he had thought this would make them disgruntled, he was disappointed. It did not. The elves had dismounted and talked among themselves, as time meant very little to a race of immortals.

The king's man was dressed in an immaculate long black robe, and his silver hair lay swept back from his high forehead. He approached the visitors humbly and begged their pardon, apparently a genuine gesture on the surface, at least.

"I am so sorry for the wait. I have been in a council meeting and only just received the message of your arrival. The messenger will be punished for not bringing me word sooner."

Aedith smiled. "It has been no bother, and the messenger can be excused."

The advisor, Victor, would not hear of it and he insisted the subject would not be dropped or forgotten.

"Come," he said as they strode into the city. The elven prince walked beside him followed by mounted soldiers and advisors.

"Welcome to Zeiglon, the mightiest city in the east," Victor stated proudly and aggressively. The elven prince remained silent.

As they walked, the prince uttered little more than diplomatic words while he was shown the buildings and the sculptures of the city. They wound their way toward the mighty castle that dominated the sky. Its many towers were dark and foreboding and reminded Aedith of rotting teeth. The local population appeared both awe-stricken and frightened as they stared at the elves in their immaculate dress accompanying the dark advisor to the king.

Before reaching the keep, the entourage passed a massive oval structure unlike any the elves had ever seen. Victor remarked that it was the coliseum where the king held horse races.

Soon they crossed a heavy drawbridge and approached the gate to the castle complex. They passed through a gatehouse where two gates stood open and above them the recessed signs of a portcullis could be seen in the ceiling. Finally they emerged into a wide courtyard.

From behind them they heard a great clang as the portcullis was dropped into place. All around them, soldiers of Zeiglon emerged, armed with bows and crossbows, all trained on the elven diplomatic mission. Victor, the king's advisor, quickly stepped away and shouted at the elves.

"I would not draw a weapon, or you all will die today."

Treacherous cretin, Aedith thought.

The elves were outnumbered and surrounded by the Zeiglon bowmen. Prince Aedith held up his hand, unbuckled his sword belt and let it fall to the stone floor of the courtyard. The rest of the elves grudgingly followed his lead.

Immediately the elven horsemen were rushed by soldiers and roughly pulled down from their saddles. All the elven soldiers were then led to a horse pen and placed within it, the enemy bows still trained on them.

Prince Aedith was treated with slightly more dignity and allowed to remain standing beside the king's advisor. Victor took him by the arm and roughly pulled the elven prince through the halls and passages of the castle complex where dark-eyed Zeiglon soldiers were always in attendance.

The prince was led to the rear of the palace and finally ended up in the empty throne room. He and Victor stood there for several clicks of the clock until, from a side door, the Emperor of Zeiglon, Zachary the First himself, waddled in.

A huge man both in height and girth, the emperor sat heavily on the infamous shell throne of Zeiglon. The throne reached three rods in height and was made entirely of seashells that fanned out behind the king like the feathers of a peacock.

"To what do I owe the pleasure of such a high dignitary as yourself, Prince Aedith?" the emperor asked.

The prince, using every ounce of his elven heritage to maintain his composure, replied, "I am here to negotiate an end to hostilities between yourself and Partha." He recognized the staff that the emperor held at that time, the reproduced Staff of Adaman, as the sign of his reign.

"Hmm," the large man muttered, "I see no end to that. I want those lands, and I will have them by force of arms. The Parthians will be destroyed."

Prince Aedith bowed. "That is but one way to settle this. There are many more possibilities that can be discussed."

The emperor waved a hand dismissing that idea.

"Victor, please escort our esteemed visitor to his suite."

"Most assuredly, master," the advisor said.

Aedith could feel the fear emanating from the man as he addressed his superior. Two guardsmen grabbed both of Aedith's arms as he turned around.

"Come," Victor beckoned.

The guards fell into step beside the advisor and they all led the elven ambassador out of the throne room and into the vast maze-like corridors of the palace.

They walked some distance before descending several flights of stairs that led below ground. Cold permeated the walls and cold water dripped from the ceiling. They came to a stout, roughly hewn door and the guard used an immense key to open it. A putrid smell wafted over them all, and Aedith was dragged into a dark chamber and heavy, rusted manacles were clapped over his wrists.

"I hope you enjoy your stay," the advisor snickered. "My master will see you when it is convenient for him."

The door slammed shut.

Although dark in the room, Aedith used his keen elven eyes to scan his surroundings. Several skeletons hung manacled along the walls, and he wondered if they too were still waiting for their audience with Emperor Zachary. Like them, Aedith was manacled to the wall with only several paces of chain in which he could move about.

Later that day — Aedith was sure at least seven turns of the clock had passed — a jailor brought him food.

"The emperor wants you to stay alive," the grungy man cackled. "You're to get a regular supply of food. Mind you, it's not what you're used to, I assure you, but it'll keep you alive."

The jailor put a wooden tray far enough away from him that the prince had to strain to reach it. The food was mashed meat of some type and moldy bread with a wooden cup of water set to the side.

The jailor watched the elf as he reached out for the food and began eating. "We'll get along just fine as long as you keep to your place. I'll be kind, but cause me any trouble, and I'll be eating your share of the food."

Well, Aedith thought, the food can't be that bad if he'll eat it. In fact, despite his delicate taste, the slop was edible and sustaining. When the jailor had gone, he finished his meal and with a small rock, scratched a line on the wall. He knew that it would be the first of many days he was to be held here.

He was right. It was several weeks into his stay before the door opened and Victor made an appearance.

CHAPTER FIVE

Far west of Zeiglon five thousand troops were now poised on the northern border of Partha, a mile from the largest of the westernmost border forts. They waited for a signal to attack. The orders had been given calling for them to take the fortress, establish control of the area, and then work their way down the chain of forts until Partha responded.

As the Parthian guard made his circuit, he kept his cloak wrapped tightly around him, the hood pulled low. He had night duty, and walking along the walls of the small, cold Parthian fort had become mind numbing.

The fortification was little more than four walls with four small towers and just enough room inside for a stable and a barracks. The installation was part of a string of fortified points along the frontier which separated the kingdoms of Zeiglon and Partha, two countries that were bitter enemies. This fort helped secure the Parthian land.

The guard walking the wall this night was Partha raised and city born. He was not used to the cold, blowing winds of the plains, and the floors of the stone fort froze his feet and added to his misery. The chain mail armor he wore under his cloak made him freeze even more.

He stopped and blew into his hands to warm them. In the quiet he heard something heavy strike the top of the stable below. He peered closer and saw one of his fellow guards lying on top of the horse enclosure. He then heard, but did not see, two arrows whistle past his head, one neatly slicing open the side of his hood and nicking the side of the helmet he wore underneath.

He ducked, ran to the nearest tower and began ringing the alarm bell. Sleepy but well-armed soldiers stumbled out of the barracks and swarmed up the stone steps to the parapet.

The attackers already had scaled the walls and established a foothold and another guard now lay dead with an arrow in his chest. A vicious fight soon took place in the narrow parapet and the Parthians pushed hard at the attackers with their shields. The enemy's swords rose and fell, striking the metal edges of the Parthian shields and releasing bright sparks as they struck against the shields or the granite blocks of the fortification.

The defenders deftly plied their spears and stabbed at the enemy troops over their shield wall. The wounded or dead were kicked unceremoniously off the parapet by the Parthian guards into the interior of the fort. Slowly the invaders were driven back to their ladders. Several tried to climb down, but the brave defenders twisted the top of their ladder and sent the attackers screaming as they fell onto the deadly spiked moat.

The alert young Parthian soldier had soon forgotten the cold as the fire arrows flew and embedded themselves in the tower roof. Flames quickly fanned out and thick smoke filled the small tower room. He had to escape.

As he sounded the ringing bell's last chime, he saw a ladder appear not three paces in front of him. The end was heavily covered in cloth to silence the noise of it striking against the granite of the fort's walls.

He stepped through the haze of smoke and ran one raider through with his sword. As the next enemy climbed the ladder, the guard struck him in the head with the hilt of his sword and killed him instantly.

Arrows began to careen off the guard's helmet and with more strength than he thought he possessed, he used a long pole with a V-shaped metal end to push the ladder away from the wall. It fell backward and landed on a mass of attackers waiting their turn to climb upward.

Help then arrived and several guards came to his aid, their arrows notched and ready, but one of the guards immediately pitched backward when an arrow pierced his throat.

Near the gate the shrouded enemies climbed through the crenellations without meeting opposition and spread out as they gained the high walkway. The commander of the fort was the first to confront them and he slashed at the first attacker, slicing through the robe he wore. The raider fell into the yard below.

The commander noted that his sword did not penetrate the enemy's robe as easily as it should have, but he had no time to contemplate why. Another robed figure had appeared before him. The commander ducked a wild swing from the attacker and then ran the man through. Soon other Parthians joined him and helped him drive the enemy back toward their ladders, and then the archers arrived on the walkways to fire at the enemy below.

The commander and his men were now cutting a bloody swath through the invaders. Several of his guards fell, but he continued pushing the robed enemies back toward their only escape route. Many of the invaders had now had enough and began climbing back down the ladders. The commander reached their escape point and when one opponent turned to hurry down the ladder, he pushed against the man's chest and sent him crashing below. The soldier on the next ladder overturned and hesitated before descending. It was a fatal mistake. In that instant the commander ran his sword through the man's throat.

From the fort's walled enclosure below the Parthian commander heard a loud "boom" at the front gate and felt the blow ripple through the granite walls. Eight enemy men with a battering ram had begun striking the gate again and again. The commander called for more archers and he heard the "boom" once more, quickly followed by another and then another.

The archers adjusted their aim and fired down at the soldiers manning the ram, but it seemed like a losing battle. Whenever one man fell, another rushed forward to take his place. The commander left the parapet and ran back down to see how well the gate was withstanding the damage.

One thick cross board had been pushed in, and he stood ready to fight if the hole opened any larger. Above him his archers now manned all four walls and fired down at the enemy. The ram struck again and cracked the wood further while heavy dust began to fall from the stone ceiling of the gatehouse.

The commander could see the attackers' hands pulling back the loose boards, and the helmeted head of one of them poked through the hole. The commander lashed out with his sword, picking off enemies as they pulled at the boards, but still, the hole grew larger.

Then came one last "boom" and it was over.

The assault had gone on for a full turn of the clock, but it suddenly ended when the sun crested the eastern sky. The invaders gathered their horses and rode quickly away from the fort.

Several of the enemy fell to the defenders' arrows before they crested the hills surrounding the fortress. Once the rest were gone and out of sight, the Parthians waited until the sun was fully up before their commander took five men to examine the fallen enemy.

He kicked over one dead raider's body and the truth came out. Hidden beneath the flowing robe, otherwise used by the traveling tribes of the grasslands, the commander recognized the armor of the Zeiglon Empire.

The Parthian soldiers were assigned to search the dead and to dispatch the wounded.

The commander called for three volunteers to each take a message of the attack to the next fort further east and from there the message would eventually reach the capital Partha. The three men rode off hard in three different directions in case any Zeiglon soldiers lay in wait to kill them.

They had now surrounded the first fort without a problem.

The next day the defenders of the fort woke to see that five hundred soldiers had surrounded them during the night, and the alarm bells were ringing. Little did they know that beyond the hill forty-five hundred more soldiers waited.

Five hundred bowmen arched their arrows upward, released them altogether and the arrows fell inside the fort. The defenders ducked below the parapets, but the sheer number of arrows, coming from all directions, decimated the Parthians. Their commander lay prone on the ground where he had fallen with two arrows in his back.

The only safe places were the corner towers, the barracks and the stables.

The attacking soldiers lit fire arrows next and let them fly. The inside of the fortress was soon an inferno. Some Parthian soldiers opened the gates to escape while others ran to the towers, but the soldiers trying to escape through the gate were mercilessly shot down.

The commander of the Zeiglon army motioned for his troops to wait for the fire to burn itself out before he ordered them to enter the fort and kill all who still survived there.

When the soldiers finally entered the fort, they were assaulted by arrows that flew from the small towers, but the projectiles hardly made a dent in the enemy soldiers. Soon the Zeiglon forces were on the ramparts and brief battles ensued at each tower, but the Parthians were quickly overwhelmed and Zeiglon troops gained control of the western portion of Partha.

The enemy soldiers immediately began expanding the fortress by bringing in large granite stones from Zeiglon mines. They also began sending large parties of mounted troops into the west of Parthia.

News of the Zeiglon attack would not reach the Parthian capital for several weeks, but even then there was nothing the Parthians could do. Their soldiers were spread too thin, and gathering a large enough force to counter the recent invasion would leave the rest of the country defenseless.

CHAPTER SIX

Aedith was asleep on the cold stone floor of his prison cell when he heard the key in the lock and the heavy creak of rusted hinges. Suddenly a torch illuminated the cell.

The jailor held the light as Victor, the king's advisor, and several guards made their way over to Aedith. Using another key the jailor unlocked the prince's manacles, and the guards grabbed him by both arms.

"Come, Prince," the advisor said. "The emperor has declared a day of celebration and wishes you to join him."

Unshackled, Aedith was led out into the bright corridors of the palace. He could see that the advisor was clearly unsettled when the daylight failed to affect his eyesight and he knew Victor was wondering if it was because of a spell the elf had cast.

Aedith was led into the courtyard. A carriage waited. Victor and the guards entered it first and the prince was handed up into their care. It was a short trip, but the curtains were drawn shut to prevent any passersby from seeing who was inside.

The carriage stopped in a low stone enclosure. Aedith was taken out of it roughly, and his keen hearing picked out the exciting murmur of people above him. He knew instantly where he was, the great oval coliseum he had seen while riding into the city.

He was led upward on finely fitted marble stairs and into the royal box overlooking the oval enclosure within the coliseum's stone walls. He was then chained to a chair several paces in front of the emperor. He faced the grounds below him.

"Ha, my friend! I welcome you to our festivities." Zachary was gloating behind Aedith. "We celebrate a victory over the forces of Partha and the annexation of some of their lands. So, you see, your mission was destined to fail from the start. This annexation was scheduled long before you departed your homeland."

The prince remained silent as he watched in horror while the troops of his elvan command, now in rags, were pushed out onto the sand covered ground and shoved unarmed from a hidden entry way. The proud elves stood their ground while the huge crowd of citizens assembled in the coliseum erupted in cheers. From another entrance chariots rushed out onto the stadium floor and Zeiglon warriors attacked the unarmed elves without provocation.

Arrows and spears flew into the elves. Some were dodged, but most of the first volleys struck true. The elves broke from their circular group and ranged around the stadium while the chariots continued to circle and attack them.

Several elves took the thrown spears and hurled them back at the passing chariots. A few struck down a driver or an accompanying warrior. Dodging the bladed chariot wheels, the elves retrieved the bows and arrows from the fallen charioteers and began attacking the enemy ranks. The soldiers of Zeiglon, however, did not play fair. From another hidden entrance more heavily armed squads joined the fray and rushed into the elves, cutting through their ranks.

The elven bowmen, still dodging the chariots, took up positions behind the overturned vehicles. Their meager defensive position allowed them to turn their fire onto the foot soldiers and soon the remaining elves all were armed from the fallen soldiers.

They fought bravely on the bloodied coliseum floor, but another doorway opened and feral beasts entered the arena. Lions from the far west country, starved and beaten by their handlers, rushed into the fray. The elves, the foot soldiers, and the people in the stands all turned their attention to these feral creatures. Around the arena the crowds stood in their seats and cheered, eagerly awaiting the bloodbath that was bound to ensue.

The elves and the Zeiglon soldiers took cover behind the chariots and began shooting at the beasts, but their arrows and spears seemed only to anger them. The lions and tigers attacked the elves and the Zeiglon soldiers and many of the beasts were cut down, but not without a heavy toll for both sides.

Several elves were mauled before the last lion fell lifeless onto the sandy floor. The elves, weren't the only ones attacked. Zeiglon foot soldiers were also the targets of the beasts and, like it or not, they took cover with the wood elves. Clearly, Zeiglon's lord and master Zachary cared little for the well-being of even his own soldiers.

By this time all the chariots had been overturned and used by the defenders to try to stay alive. Men and elves cowered together for safety. A hundred gladiators, trained specially to fight in the great coliseum, now entered the fray and quickly closed with the remaining elves and men.

The elvish bowmen again took their toll on their new attackers, but the gladiators closed the distance between them and the defenders, and the fight was on. The unarmed elves relied on their quickness, but this little fazed the hardened gladiators. The human charioteers and soldiers were quickly dispatched, and the elves were surrounded. Their arrows ran out as the gladiators closed in on them.

The elves attacked with one last charge, bearing the discarded arms from the fallen humans or their bare hands if no other weapons were available. A melee ensued but the gladiators prevailed until only a few elves were left panting in the middle of the killing grounds.

That brief pause did little to calm the crowd who were still caught up in their blood lust. Prince Aedith watched it all, but was unwilling to let the emperor see his true emotions while his fellow elves were slaughtered before him. Inside, his heart and soul were torn asunder. Only such complete devastation of their bodies could kill his fellow elves.

The emperor leaned forward, a scented cloth over his nose and mouth.

"Your soldiers fought well," he said.

He made a signal and the gladiators below backed away a dozen paces. The wounded elves were now ringed about by these professional killers. The crowd finally quieted.

The emperor watched on serenely. Then he whispered to Victor, who hurried down the stairs and out to a slender platform. The crowd hushed. They knew the emperor was about to speak.

"Hear the emperor," Victor shouted. "These elves are to be spared. They are to take a message to their homeland that we hold their proud prince as hostage to keep them from meddling in our business."

There were a few mumblings in the crowd from those who wanted more blood.

"Enough," he yelled, "It is the will of the emperor."

A hushed silence settled over the spectators as the remaining elves—a mere dozen—were led by the gladiators off the bloody sand into the depths of the coliseum. Aedith was unshackled from his chair amid catcalls from the crowd and escorted out of the arena to a waiting carriage that would take him back to his lightless cell.

Several days later, still in the pure darkness of his cell, the prince was startled when a light began to coalesce in front of him. The figure of a man was revealed wearing immaculate white robes with a serene look upon his face.

"I am Adaman, god and protector of this world," the figure said. "I have come to instruct you."

Aedith was at a loss for words. A god had appeared in his prison...and not an elven god, but a human one. Could this be a trick, a farce put on for Zachary's own pleasure?

Even for Aedith's own long-lived race, this was unusual.

"Do not worry yourself over such trivial things, Prince Aedith," Adaman assured him. "I am here to offer advice and a means to rid this world of the evil that Zeiglon has become. Because of her jealousy, my twin sister has manipulated this kingdom for her own evil purposes."

Adaman sat down in the filth next to the prince and leaned against the grime encrusted wall, although it could not touch him or soil his garments. Instead, his holiness burned the filth away and left the area where it had been pristine and slightly glowing.

"To end this reign of evil," Adaman continued, "my staff must be reassembled, and only one of pure spirit can do thus."

"Am I such a pure spirit?" Aedith asked.

"Yes," Adaman replied. "There will come a time when you will be given a chance to seize the staff and the orb. Once you have them, the staff of Adaman will reform to its true shape and power. Then you must fight Zachary, the emperor who also yields the Staff of Adois. It will be a difficult task and cause much change and violence to this world. Nevertheless, it cannot be helped. An end must be put to this growing pestilence, and so it must be done. I mourn for what my world has become. You are the only one who can save it."

"I accept this mission and will do as you ask," Aedith pledged. He was humbled by Adaman's request, and he immediately became intent on his new mission.

"Remember the fate of the world lies with you," the god told him. "Fear not, for I will be there with you."

As soon as he finished speaking, the figure slowly dimmed and then was gone from the dungeon.

CHAPTER SEVEN

Emperor Zachary sat at his conference table with his closest advisors and pointed at a map of Partha.

"Are the plans in action?" he asked.

"Yes, milord," his senior general answered. "The troops are assembling along the border and should be ready in six months for a full-scale invasion, your eminence. Our troops already control the western outposts. In fact, our weak enemies have allowed us to run roughshod over the west. The Parthians will suspect nothing. A full-scale attack into their heartland and their capital will come as a complete surprise. Of course, utmost secrecy is being observed."

"Good," the emperor replied. "The only allies they could possibly employ are those dwarves to the north."

"My lord, the dwarves are fragmented and pose no threat," an aide assured him.

Zachary slammed his fist on the table. "I will decide who or what poses a threat. I will not allow even the smallest possibility to endanger this campaign. We will overrun Partha with ease, but there still is a potential ally to the north. I want no one to escape our invasion, even if it means killing every one of those dwarves, too. If the Parthians retreat into the mountains, they will forever be a thorn in our side." He looked around at each and every man. "So how do we deal with the dwarves?"

"Can we not attack them to keep their forces occupied?" one soldier asked.

"No, that would alert the Parthians," Zachary said. "Although it is an admirable plan, their natural enemies are the orcs. Perhaps…we might be able to use them. They are as greedy as a Parthian merchant. If we find the most powerful tribe and spread gold among its members, we may be able to persuade the orcs to attack the dwarves. It should be easy if they just concentrate on one city at a time. We will send a company of riders, dressed as mercenaries, west then north to find the most desirable tribes among those foul beasts. The force must be large enough to cower the orcs and yet still skirt Partha without arousing any suspicion."

Over the next few days, their plans were finalized and a troop of one hundred horsemen wearing mismatched clothing and armor were readied. The tack on the horses was also changed from any regulated design to prevent outsiders from discovering that the men were from Zeiglon. The captain picked for the duty was a short, thin man, weather-beaten from living his life in the saddle.

He met with the Zeiglon general who outlined the plans and gave him two pack horses loaded with saddlebags filled with gold. The company left the castle in the dark of night for the long ride west and then north. Anyone who noticed them would have thought the troop was just another of the emperor's hired fighters.

The going was easy once they had left the forested hills of Zeiglon and had entered the grassy plains of Partha. There they picked up speed and were soon so far west that only a long-range patrol of Parthians could ever spot them.

As the Zeiglon troops neared the foothills of the northern mountains, one of their scouts came riding hard back to the captain, pointing back the way they had come.

"Riders have picked up our trail. They look to number no more than fifty. Probably a long-range patrol from Partha."

The captain considered his scout's words.

"Alright, we stay on course and let them catch up. Remember, we aren't from Zeiglon. We're just mercenaries going north. There is no reason to fight these men. To do so would alert Partha to our presence. Nonetheless, if we are forced to fight, they can have no survivors."

The Parthians closed the gap and finally caught up with the mercenary band early that afternoon. Circling around the suspicious troop, they stopped in front of them and blocked their way. The Parthian soldiers wore light mail and bore long lances along with an assortment of smaller weapons. The leader of the Parthians rode forward and met the Zeiglon captain.

"What brings such a large force through Parthian lands?" he asked.

"We are riding north in search of employment," the captain replied. "Zeiglon has so many soldiers in their army that they have no need for a mercenary band such as ours. We seek our fortune elsewhere."

The Parthian scratched the stubble of his shaved scalp under his helmet. "Are you certain that is your tale? You could be spies from Zeiglon, passing through the west as you make your way east into our heartland."

The company commander shrugged.

"If we were, my men would have attacked you as soon as you approached. We're just restless men going about our business."

"Then you shouldn't mind my men looking through those saddlebags on your pack animals."

The captain pretended to swat a nonexistent fly buzzing about his head. It was a prearranged signal. Behind the Parthians, a dozen archers rose out of the grass, drew their bows, and sent a barrage of arrows flying into the rear of the Parthian troop. Six fell dead. The mercenaries drew their weapons and charged the rest.

The Parthian defenders barely got their lances down to charge before the Zeiglon horses slammed into them. Lances skewered Zeiglon soldiers while Parthians were struck from the saddle by a myriad of weapons. The lancers then rid themselves of their long unwieldy weapons, drew swords and began dueling rider to rider.

The Parthians were not in a close formation and soon all the horsemen were tangled in a true mêlée. Many fell, swords swung back and forth and the outnumbered defenders tried to keep their attackers at bay. But the odds were against them. Soon each Parthian fighter was surrounded and struck down from his saddle. Once on the ground they found it impossible to survive as the Zeiglon horsemen rode over the wounded soldiers.

Several Parthians tried to ride away to freedom, but the mercenaries shot them from their saddles with flights of arrows. In the end all fifty Parthians were dead, but only seventeen Zeiglon raiders had lost their lives.

True to their nature, the victors took the Parthian horses and ruthlessly looted the bodies before continuing their journey north.

When the Zeiglon soldiers reached the foothills of the Mordolwyn Mountains, they searched for an orc village or for anyone else who could direct them in the right direction. After a few weeks of travel and tracking, they eventually found their way to a village that contained a mixture of orcs, goblins, and several ogres, all living in the one enclave.

The village had a stout tree trunk wall that encircled it and a single gate, and as the Zeiglon soldiers approached, the villagers scampered back inside the safety of their walled compound and shut the gate. The Zeiglon captain rode up to the gate and used the age-old method of attaching a white flag to his spear.

It worked. He wasn't shot out of his saddle, and he realized his gut feeling had been right. He began to feel better about dealing with the strange creatures inside.

One orc stood behind the gate and by the look of his feathered cape and conical hat, he was a shaman.

"What you want, human?" he yelled out.

"I need a scout," the captain replied. "I'm searching for only the strongest tribe of orcs to do business with. I will pay, and you have my word for the safety of the scout."

The shaman conferred with several orcs and goblins behind him before calling back. "What do we get if we lend you one of our fighters?"

"I will pay the village for the use of the scout," he answered.

The village kept its gates closed while they conferred. Before long, a large eyed orc came forward and approached the captain.

"I take you to Stilko, a brave orc who commands many warriors and villages, but first show me gold."

The captain nodded his head and tossed down a pouch that chinked loudly.

"This is for the shaman."

The orc brought the parcel inside and when he returned, he was armored in rough hides with a wickedly curved sword on his hip. He looked up at the horseman.

"My gold?" and asked.

A smaller bag of coins was tossed down. "Ten to start. Forty more once you get us to this Stilko."

The orc's protruding eyes bulged as he caught the small pouch.

"I will take you. Come." He began a loping run back past the horsemen and they hurriedly turned to catch up with him.

The company followed the orc as he continued to run, sometimes through open countryside and sometimes through thick forests. He often used a trail, but sometimes he plunged off the road or the path altogether and the horsemen had trouble following in single file after the fleet-footed orc.

At night the orc stayed to himself away from the humans and made a rock ringed fire and he cooked small animals he had killed on his run during the day. The riders had been surprised how sure handed he was with a stone in bringing down his dinner. He would pull a stone from a belt pouch and, barely slowing to a stop, throw it at a squirrel. He seldom missed and he always recovered his throwing stones after killing the animal.

Five days later, they approached a village even smaller than the one their guide had come from. It wasn't fortified and as the soldiers approached, the orcs gathered their weapons, ready to meet the horsemen.

The hired scout ran ahead and, after a brief discussion, returned to the horsemen. The sweat-drenched orc pointed northeast.

"The villagers say that Stilko's main village is that way, several days run. I must warn you that Stilko is an evil orc and commands many warriors. I would advise against going to him for help. But, come, we go."

The orc was soon running full tilt down a wooded path. Again the horsemen had trouble keeping up with him and barely avoided the tree limbs on the awkward rock-strewn path. They kept the nimble orc in sight throughout the day.

That night the orc came over to the captain's fire and stood before him, fidgeting. "May I speak?"

The captain motioned him to sit on the ground opposite him.

"Of course, my friend."

The orc sat cross-legged. "My lord, this is a dangerous thing you do. Don't trust Stilko. He will kill all of you and keep the gold for himself."

The captain waved away the comment. "I have more than enough gold to keep his interest and I can still safeguard myself and my men."

The orc looked down into the flames. "You do not know where we go. His village covers much of a valley and he has five hundred fighters. He can call four times more than that, as well, and take your gold and kill your men."

"What is it you would have me do?" the captain asked sternly.

"Run," the orc advised him. "Take the gold and go east to the human lands. Best choice for you to live."

"No," the captain said. "I have my orders, and I intend to carry them out."

"Then give me my pay before you enter Stilko's camp, and I'll be off," the orc said.

The next day, as the forest began to open up, the orc slowed his pace and kept a close eye on his surroundings. On either side of the horsemen, several hundred paces off the path, rode a long line of orcs. The captain's scout halted the column and pointed to a valley ahead where they saw smoke from many fires.

"That is village," their guide said. "Give me my gold now. I leave."

The captain tossed a small pouch of gold down to the orc, and without a moment's hesitation their guide was off and running back the way they had come. The captain watched him go and waved the company forward.

The orc horsemen kept pace with them as they crested the hill.

A lump formed in the captain's throat. This was no mere village. It was a city. Its buildings and roads were unorganized, but it had stout walls and watchtowers. It looked like at least two thousand inhabitants resided in the enclave, and the captain wondered if he shouldn't have listened to the guide. If they hadn't been shadowed by the orc calvary, he might have taken his scout's warning and headed east, forgetting about the mission.

As it was, knowing how evil his emperor Zachary was and what would happen to him if he gave up his mission, the captain realized he had little choice.

They were soon surrounded by orcs as the captain and his troops wound their way down the hill toward Stilko's city.

The captain arranged his men in a defensive circle and waited. He had caused quite a stir among the orcs at the gate. Several of the horsemen who had been shadowing them rode quickly past them and down into the city.

A single turn of the clock passed before a large group of orcs marched through the streets and issued forth from the gate in front of the captain and his men. Judging from a distance, the captain estimated about two hundred foot soldiers were now gathered before the hill in front of him. The riders that had been following them had all disappeared from view.

In front of the advancing troop one huge orc in black plate mail rode back and forth on a massive black horse over eighteen hands high.

"If this goes bad, be prepared to retreat as fast as possible," the captain called to his men.

Finally, the foot soldiers before them began to advance through the high grass at the bottom of the hill. The orcs, wearing some semblance of uniforms, then lined up before the waiting soldiers. The huge orc leader reared up in his saddle.

"Why you come here, humans?" he asked.

The Zeiglon captain rode part way down and yelled, "I bring a message from my master to the great Stilko."

The orc laughed. "I be Stilko, but why care I about your master?"

"I come at the behest of the Emperor of Zeiglon," the captain said in return.

"So what? Your emperor be nothing. I master here," Stilko said. The orcs behind him beat their weapons on their shields.

"My master wishes to seek your counsel concerning the dwarves."

The silence that followed was palpable. Stilko thought about what had been said and finally spoke.

"I meet you halfway up hill."

The two rode to a halfway point, and the captain was astonished when he saw how the orc deported himself. Stilko, his open-faced helmet held under his arm, showed himself to be a clean-cut orc. His hairy scalp was neatly brushed. There was no foul odor about him, but instead there was a sweetness in the air, as if the large orc had used some spice to clear his smell.

All the civilities stopped, though, when he shot out his first words.

"I no trust black emperor's lackeys."

The captain hid his own anger well.

"My lord Stilko, I ask that you listen to my master's proposal. The dwarves are weak. Spread across the hills and mountains in small cities, they do not cooperate with one another. If you would invade in the east, they will fall to your army, easily, one at the time."

Stilko waved a hand. "I think of this before. Why now?"

"My lord wishes to attack Partha, and the dwarves might aid them. That was why he sent me with a generous payment...so that you might do him the favor. It is a favor that will greatly increase your status and your wealth."

The orc scratched at his chin. "How much gold your emperor send?"

The captain knew that if they were to be attacked, it would happen now. He flashed a signal to one of his men to bring up the two horses with heavily laden saddlebags.

"My lord wishes to give you this to aid in your command. I and my men are also at your disposal." The last was a lie but if it saved his men, it was a worthwhile lie.

Stilko thought about the proposition for a single click of the clock before speaking.

"Be much loot in dwarven villages. I lead soldiers over the mountains, but no need help."

With that, he drew his sword and in one swift movement plunged it into the unsuspecting captain.

That was the signal to the orc bowman who had slipped close to the Zeiglon horsemen and they unleashed a volley of arrows. The riders jerked and fell from their horses, dead or wounded, and their animals neighed and reared in pain as the arrows struck home.

Suddenly, from the cover of the surrounding forest, another horde of orcs charged. There was no cohesion between them or disciplined battle lines, just a mad rush of orc flesh toward the band of Zeiglon men.

Stilko retreated back into his two hundred soldiers, and they all drew their bows and aimed at the remaining humans at the top the hill.

The humans had to struggle to get their horses under control as the orc hosts struck home. The mounted Zeiglon slashed right and left, severing arms and heads, while the orcs tried to pull them from their horses. Many of the orcs reeled away with grievous wounds and the Zeiglon horsemen used their hand guards and hilts to knock aside their attackers.

Many of the horsemen charged straight over the hilltop to escape the orcs, only to be met by a hail of arrows. Most of them toppled from their horses, but several turned, trying to escape across the top of another hill, but many of these fell to orc arrows. Only a few escaped.

Meanwhile the rest of the horsemen fought on. Some dismounted, their swords ringing on their attackers shields and thrusting into or hacking away at the orcs' flesh, but the end was inevitable. The orcs drove the men into a center ring and shot arrow after arrow into the final defenders, bringing them down one by one.

When no humans were left alive, their horses were rounded up and Stilko inspected the saddlebags, pleased with the gold they contained.

He thought how impertinent the humans were, thinking they could manipulate him with gold. He would have attacked the dwarves himself, eventually, and in fact had been planning such a move for years. Those dirty little dwarf miners had plenty of gold and gems, and his followers would only be too pleased to sack their villages.

This Zeiglon gold had just sped up his timetable. It was enough for him to now gather an army together and strike east toward the dwarven treasures.

Unbeknownst to the orcs, a dwarf and a half elf had watched the battle from a well concealed position. Stilko held the saddle bags aloft, and the dwarf knew trouble was coming to his eastern kin.

He had another mission to complete before taking care of that business, though. Besides, he had time. The mountain passes to the east were still clogged with snow and it would be well into spring before they began to thaw. Unfortunately, that also left the orc leader more time to gather troops from the outlying villages and create a formidable army.

Making sure the orcs were searching to the south for the few still missing horsemen, the dwarf motioned to his partner and they slid silently backward to their mountain horses, mounted them and sped north.

After the battle Stilko summoned his officers to his hall. The gigantic room was one hundred paces long, made from smooth wooden planks and had two large stone fireplaces. Straw covered the floor. Trophies from his past victories lined the walls. Many orc and goblin banners hung there, too, along with weapons of various kinds.

Stilko sat in a high-backed chair at a long table that could seat twenty. His officers gathered around the table and took their seats.

"Well done today," Stilko began, speaking in their native language instead of the broken human one. "We will feast well on human flesh tonight."

The others banged their fists in approval on the table, but their leader silenced them.

"I have a plan that might interest all of you," Stilko said. "In the spring when the mountain passes begin to clear, we will head east and raid the dwarven villages."

The pleasure of his commanders showed again in their eager faces.

"We will summon my vassals and create an army that none shall stand against. The long beards will be overrun, and all their treasures will be ours," Stilko shouted. He let the noise of his shouting officers continue for several clicks of the clock before waving them to silence. "We must prepare for winter, but you also must prepare your soldiers. You will be the first ones to take the villages...and therefore the better share of the loot." He saw the hungry looks among his commanders and he added, "Of course, I intend to get my share as well."

There was laughter all around the table.

Stilko brought out the human captain's saddlebag and spilled the pouches of gold out onto the table.

"Take this as a generous gift from me and see to your soldiers. They should be well cared for this winter and they will soon see what benefits they will receive in the coming campaign."

Shouts of joy erupted as the pouches were passed down the table.

"This is only for the betterment of your soldiers," Stilko reminded them severely. "Should I find that you are ill-treating my soldiers, you will be killed in a most painful way."

CHAPTER EIGHT

T he wizard Melgor was an assistant to Brill, the keeper of Dragon Isle's library. It was a job he had held for many boring years, but at least it afforded him access to certain powerful books kept under lock and key.

Melgor had heard Maliki, one of his masters, speaking to Brill one day of the potential of a certain student and how they expected great things from him since the young apprentice had first entered the academy. After learning of his masters' interest in Celedant, he had followed Celedant's rising star.

Melgor had observed Celedant going freely about the academy and that made him jealous as well as angry. Melgor himself had been studying for countless years, but he had risen no higher than an assistant to the librarian.

The reason was easy to explain. Even at that moment, for instance, he was studying a copy of demon summoning which he had secreted from the library's special collection. It was deemed too dark for the students and only to be used by certain masters.

Had they known he had taken it, Melgor would have been punished severely.

The fates had been unkind to Melgor…or so he thought. He had attempted to summon a demon, but it was an unmitigated disaster. That had been years ago. Certain now that he was better at summoning, he decided to have another go at it. Having read and reread almost all the books in the library on the subject, he had learned an important lesson: demons were extremely hard to bind to your will.

Still, one night, he attempted to summon a demon on a secluded section of the local beach. Meticulously he drew the correct runes in the sand and began the summoning spell. The vortex the books had described appeared and an angry demon, three rods tall with mottled pustules covering its body, came out and rushed the runes that held the spell.

He appeared on the beach just short of the wizard.

Melgor was terrified – more than he had ever been in his life – and it showed on his face. The demon laughed at him from behind the magical runes, its smile a mouth full of rotting teeth. Melgor then tried to cast a binding spell and for a single click of the clock, the demon was seized. He could feel himself gaining control of the creature, but Melgor's control was short-lived.

The demon snapped the spell and laughed again, its voice deep and gravelly.

"Fool! Thou canst not bind me."

His fear now forgotten; Melgor now was furious. He began the ritual to send the demon back where it had come from, but before he could finish, a wave rushed high up the beach and over a section of runes, washing them away.

The demon let out a triumphant bellow and attacked, lifting up the foolish wizard and throwing him ten paces into the water. The water was deep enough to cushion his landing and, recovering quickly, he cast a lightning spell and blasted the demon in the chest, sorely wounding it.

The creature from hell was not finished yet. As Melgor rose above the water and moved toward shore, he cast a spell that sent a purple pulse that knocked the demon backwards. As it fell, Melgor continued his attack, but the battle had begun to take its toll on the summoning wizard himself.

The demon was forced further backward until its back was against the jagged seawall of the beach, where it could not escape. Melgor had gone mad with battle lust, and the use of such magic was driving him to a frenzy. Spell after spell beat down the demon and left it huddled down against the beach with a mass of wounds.

Melgor walked over to it triumphantly. "Laugh at me. Will you? Thought you were so powerful that you could destroy me?" He laughed harshly. "You'd have been better off to become my servant."

Raising his hands, Melgor conjured one last spell that sent the demon back to the nine hells. As it blinked from its existence on the beach, a cloud of black soot was all that remained and it drifted through the ocean breeze and out to sea.

Coming down from his fevered high, Melgor was hit with a realization. From this point on, he was no longer a wizard. He was now a warlock. What should he do? He was sure to be banished should this be discovered.

He quickly erased all traces of what had happened, but it was too late. The Masters had felt the secret but powerful use of magic on the island and they sent a party of battle wizards and men-at-arms to bring the miscreant back to Edain.

The Masters were still unaware of Melgor's change in status, but seeing his excessive use of magic told them that he could not show proper restraint. They restricted him to the interior of the keep, but kept him as Brill's assistant so that the librarian could keep a closer eye on him. They had deemed it was better to shut him away from the daylight.

Nevertheless, Melgor still studied summoning whenever possible, although more secretively and carefully.

Years had passed, and other than reading numerous forbidden texts—no matter how obscure—Melgor had refrained from dabbling in the forbidden arts. As he grew older, he realized how naïve he had been at the art as a younger wizard. He might have overcome his misstep and once more become a wizard, but alas, he felt that his new understanding and constant studies would better enable him in the future to summon a demon, but control it.

Now, however, Celedant was always in the library, and the masters were constantly brandishing complements on the young wizard. Their praise of the new wizard made Melgor abysmally ill.

He knew that at some point, he would cross paths with the younger wizard. It was only a matter of time before he left the academy and made his own way into the world outside the Isle. Once he was on his own, Melgor thought that his power would garner him fame and fortune. He would be free to practice his arts. That was why he studied. That was the only desire that drove Melgor.

Nevertheless, if anything, his secret activity made him more aware of those around him who would seek to end his studies. There were rumors of wizards going black, as they said, turning to evil spells and studies. If they had only known what shutting Melgor up in the library had done to him. It had made him powerful beyond his wildest imagination…at least, in theory. He still stopped short of a true summoning since he was no longer as rash as he had been in the old days.

Celedant would be the masters' best choice to send after him when he left to be on his own. Melgor knew he was too powerful to be allowed to practice his arts as he himself willed. They would send their best, and that would be Celedant. Only for that reason did Melgor stay in the library. Keep your enemies near was a lesson he had learned early on in his studies.

Soon it would be time to leave the Isles and he could seek his own fortune. He had exhausted his studies in the library, and he knew that there were other tomes of demonology that existed off the island and those were volumes that he longed to read. It was hinted, for instance, that the dark mages of Zeiglon had a vast collection, and Melgor's imagination often turned toward that far place.

He had to leave soon or his courage would lag. He might not take the next step. He would depart shortly, he decided, but always with an eye out for Celedant. He knew he would be his main antagonist in the years to come.

It was now several months since Melgor had left Dragon Isle, and he was ensconced in Zeiglon voraciously reading all the texts on demonology that he could get his hands on.

He quickly learned that in the wide world, one did not foolishly summon demons. He had heard and read about those warlocks that had disappeared off the face of Muiria during their studies. He would not make that mistake. Although the urge was strong, and he was sure he could control a demon, Melgor waited and studied and studied.

Living in the outside world had not been kind to him. Melgor had used his magic to some success in the human kingdoms and had eventually traveled to Zeiglon. Self-taught warlocks were a dime a dozen there, and only the most talented were making it anywhere in life. Melgor's studies on Dragon Isle gave him a leg up on most of the warlocks living in the metropolis, but he had only enough gold to rent a small house when he began his studies.

One day he heard a rumor from a former wizard of the Isle turned warlock that Celedant was soon to be released upon the world. Melgor left Zeiglon at once and made his way north.

He eventually ended up in Mount Kern, a small city-state in the east near the Mordolwyn Mountains. Once there he rented a small house in the countryside and prepared to call forth a demon.

One night he drew designs in chalk upon the wooden floor to call forth a demon and hold it in place. Melgor began the incantation and the wind around the house stirred, blowing open windows, snuffing out candles and plunging the room into darkness. He continued the spell and soon red light began forming a vortex in the middle of the sigils he had drawn.

A figure stepped out of the red glow and stood before him, a dark-hued, man-like demon, hugely muscled, with bright yellow eyes that bore down on Melgor. It wore dark clothing that matched his skin. The warlock did not flinch. He knew he could not show weakness to the demon so he stood firm.

"What is your name?" Melgor asked him.

The demon answered in a dignified voice. "I am Enth. Why have you trapped me thus?"

Melgor looked hard at him. "I have need of you. There is a man that I would have you deal with, a fledgling wizard named Celedant. I want him dead."

"Where is this wizard?" Enth asked matter of factly.

"He'll be at Trondheim or on the road south," Melgor replied. He cast a quick spell that showed Celedant, his appearance hovering in mid-air in front of Enth.

"What do I get for killing this man?" the demon asked.

"Your freedom, of course," Melgor replied smugly.

Enth charged the warlock, but ran into an invisible wall that protected Melgor. The demon howled in rage at his captor. His eyes blazed bright yellow.

"Remember, I cast a binding spell on you," the warlock threatened. "You should not waste your energy trying to attack me. Save it for the wizard Celedant."

"I will do your bidding, but when I'm finished, I will come for you!" the demon shouted.

"I doubt that," Melgor said. "I bound you to my will, and I shall cast you back to the nine hells should you attack me."

The demon growled, but knew its own fate. It vanished from the room, leaving a cold chill that caused the hair on the back of the warlock's neck to stand on end.

CHAPTER NINE

Celedant and Azimuth, who had secretly transformed into elven form, had never before set foot off Dragon Isle.

Now they were sailing south to the rocky shores of the lands of the Northmen. The seas were rough all year long, and the wizard felt queasy as the ship rocked around him. Azimuth barely seemed fazed by the rolling ship, but Celedant, dressed in thick woolen pants and several shirts, was bundled up in his cloak to keep the freezing cold out.

He tried to concentrate on his first contact with the rest of the world and tried to remember how Capres had set him down in the old wizard's study and detailed his mission.

"You are to sail to Trondheim and find the Broken Tap Inn. There you will meet Goran, a dwarf, who will be your guide. Goran will take you and Azimuth south to the dwarvan clans where you will try to help some of the clans to band together," Capres said.

"Aren't the dwarves a solitary race?" Celedant asked.

"Yes, and they probably always will be. But if they band together, they would be better prepared to meet the threat from the growing orc population. The gold that the dwarves so prize is a natural magnet to the orcs, as well as are the mines and the dark places beneath the ground where the orcs like to make their dens."

Celedant was optimistic that the clans would see the rising danger and at least start cooperating instead of remaining isolated and being easy prey for the orcs and the other monsters that lurked in the Mordolwyn mountains, not to mention the infamously nasty humans from Zeiglon.

The next morning the ship sailed away with Celedant and Azimuth on it. Eventually, it arrived in the Trondheim harbor and, mercifully for the young wizard, he stepped onto solid land again.

The Broken Tap was easily found. Almost everyone knew of the inn, but warned Celedant of the fees that the owner charged.

He and Azimuth approached the nicely painted inn with a large stable next to it. The wooden siding on it was painted a gleaming white too, and they entered the main building. There were no patrons in the public section of the inn at this early hour.

Celedant paid two gold pieces for two of the cheaper rooms and he and Azimuth, as an elf, took a single room with a bed and a dresser. It felt much better to Celedant than the cold cell that he had recently called home. He thought that Goran would not make an appearance until luncheon or dinner so he lay down to rest from the arduous sea voyage while Azimuth stood guard. As a dragon, even in his elven form, he needed less sleep and could remain awake for long periods of time.

As Celedant later descended the stairs to eat his mid-day meal, he was quick to recognize Goran. The master had described him in detail. The red-headed dwarf sat in a corner booth, so he could watch for the wizard coming in the door. He had plaited his beard into two braids that reached his chest, but even indoors he still wore his metal helmet and he had a double-bladed axe leaning against the wall within easy reach.

Goran wore leather armor with rings of metal sewn on the outside and his ruddy face bore testament to years of living outdoors. He had a scar across his forehead, starting from the right hairline and running down across to the left side and ending just above his eye. Celedant thought he had a roguish look and advanced slowly toward the dwarf. He had not expected Capres to provide such a ruffian as a guide.

Sitting next to Goran was a woman with a sturdy bow leaning against her chair and a quiver of arrows near at hand.

They both stood as the wizard and Azimuth neared and with a bright smile, the dwarf spoke.

"Well, ye must be the younglings from the Isle." He laughed at Celedant's shocked face and continued. "Don't let me appearance deceive ye. Yes, I've had a rough life for over two hundred and some odd years and there's a bit of wear and tear on the old body. Come sit. This is Gwendolyn, a half elf from the borders of Korvanna."

Celedant was surprised at the open and lighthearted speech coming from such a disreputable looking figure. He wondered for a second if this was indeed the Goran he was sent to find. The dwarf motioned with his hand now for them to sit and with a jovial smile called for the proprietor to bring food and drink.

Once seated next to the strange creature, Celedant found that he could not help but like the weather-beaten dwarf. He had a ready smile and a fair voice that belied his outer appearance. Celedant was also taken aback by the beauty of the blond archer who sat silently next to the dwarf.

Goran explained his companion's dilemma.

"Gwendolyn here was cursed by a warlock, never to speak again. But she's right good with hand signals. Ye two will have to learn them for she travels with me."

After the food arrived, the dwarf laid out his plans.

"We'll be heading south in the morning, bright and early. I've got me and Gwendolyn rooms here and will have everything ready to go. We'll be following the south road to the interior of the north lands, but then it will become all trails to the south. Not much road building down there. The dwarves are too busy fighting themselves and the monsters around what they call their homes. They have trails to the human lands for their trade goods, but that's about it. The union of human city states in the east and Partha are their main trading partners."

The archer slapped the dwarf on the arm and began hand signaling to him. He nodded his head.

"Yes, I'll tell them about the dangers the northern land holds." He looked at Celedant and continued. "The north harbors all sorts monsters, so we'll ride fast to get to the more civilized lands around the dwarvan controlled mountains. Once there, we'll cut across the trails and head for the valley of the Stonesplitter lands. And once there, ye can work yer magic to try and at least get them to sign a treaty to repel the orcs. There are always rumors out of Partha of invasions from Zeiglon. Perhaps we can go to Partha and see what trouble we can get into. Don't care for those horrid humans out of Zeiglon, but them Parthians are right nice."

Gwendolyn nodded and quickly began signing. Goran translated.

"The warlock who cursed her is from Zeiglon. She wants to go there and kill him."

"Understandable," Azimuth said.

Goran continued with his thoughts as their food came and in between mouthfuls, he told them more about the south. Afterward, they separated, Goran and Gwendolyn to purchase needed supplies, Celedant and Azimuth to look around the town and talk to some of the people there.

That night they met again and dined together. The dwarf regaled Celedant and Azimuth with stories about the lands they would pass through. Celedant thought that Goran and Gwendolyn felt safe enough traveling the trails, but he himself was having second thoughts and the safety of Dragon Isle and his cell were calling painfully to him. This would be the first time he and Azimuth would have to face real danger.

The next day dawned cold as they mounted their stout mountain horses. Trailing their two pack mules, they set off, heading south.

Chapter Ten

Warlocks usually weren't born on Dragon Isle. On the rare occasion when that happened, they were only revealed as such in training and escorted off the Isle. Otherwise, warlocks came from all over the world, and Zeiglon was known as a safe haven for them to practice their evil ways.

One particular warlock, Halsbred, was born in Zeiglon and had grown quite powerful. He had made of point of being aware of the comings and goings of various younger wizards across the lands and the mission Celedant was now attempting had become of some interest to him. That mission should have been one for a more seasoned wizard, but the fact that he was so young spoke volumes about what the masters thought of the young prodigy.

Halsbred was recruited by the Zeiglon Court to spy and send reports back to the emperor, should anything unusual occur. Halsbred infiltrated the Dragon Isle and was one of Zeiglon's most important spies. A united dwarvan people might have offered Zeiglon a natural enemy, but it gave the Parthians a potential ally. Halsbred was worried. The time it would take a message to reach Zeiglon and then come back with an answer would be too long. He had to act quickly to garner information or he would have to deal outright with the upstart wizard.

Travel to Trondheim was not difficult. Arriving there secretly, however, was a problem and Halsbred paid a well-known captain to turn a blind eye and ferry him across the northern sea. Several days later, he docked in Trondheim. Two days behind Celedant, he would have to push hard to get ahead of the wizard.

Finding the right men to accompany him was, again, easy with the gold he had sequestered away. He simply went to the right places and recruited men he knew could do the job. He trusted none of them, but they were each handy with a blade and not afraid to use it. He handed out pouches of gold and promised they would receive double that amount at the end of their mission. Little did they know that they would never see the rest of the gold. Halsbred would leave none alive to tell their tale.

If word ever reached Dragon Isle of what he was doing for Zeiglon, the masters and wizards who oversaw Edain would hold him responsible and quickly exile him from his cozy position. He dared not use magic too soon for fear that the wizards of the Isle would get wind of one of their own going rogue. To camouflage himself he dressed as a Northman in front of the mercenaries he had hired.

It took just a few questions in Trondheim for him to ascertain that a wizard, a dwarf and two wood elves had left the city together and were heading down the south road toward the Mordolwyn Mountains. Halsbred did not want to go after them until they were off the road and in the wilds. The less people knew, the better.

He and his mercenary band road hard after the foursome. With Celedant and his companions ahead of them, Halsbred wanted to pass them before turning back to attack. At this point, he realized, his mission would need to go beyond mere spying on Celedant and his companions in order to be successful in the eyes of the Zeiglon authorities and in order for him to remain in their good graces.

After four days of constant riding and driving his horses to the edge of their endurance, Halsbred's point man rode back to the others. He reigned in beside the warlock and spoke hurriedly.

"There is a campfire ahead, tended by two men, a woman, and a dwarf. Though it could be the wood elves, but I'm not certain. I could only get so close to their camp."

Halsbred stroked the stubble on his face and made a quick decision.

"We'll ride around them through the forest. Come, let's go." The warlock muttered a simple spell that showed him a twisted path that led them around his prey.

The mercenaries were impressed. They figured that Halsbred was a warlock because they knew they would never have been able to wind their way through the dense forest without some kind of magical help. Like prisoners escaping from jail, they traveled at full speed, galloping to gain miles ahead of Celedant in order to pick the perfect place for an ambush.

Barely a day passed after Celedant, Azimuth, Gwendolyn and Goran had left from Trondheim when their tracks were picked up by the demon, Enth.

Sent by Melgor, Enth had run day and night, faster than anything living on Muiria. When it reached the outskirts of Trondheim, Enth could spot the unearthly glow of Celedant's passage and it immediately took up the chase.

Goran had just finished feeding the horses, and Gwendolyn was scraping out the dirt from one of the horses' hooves. While Azimuth and Celedant readied their dinner, the yellow-eyed demon Enth finally caught up with them.

He circled the camp, his footfalls unnoticed in the quiet of the evening. He could make out his quarry and he bided his time. A small amount of light still filtered down through the evergreens and it he waited for the perfect opportunity. The horses became fidgety, trying unsuccessfully to alert their masters that danger was near.

When it was completely dark, the demon decided to strike.

Celedant was sitting on a log when he felt the presence of pure evil near their camp.

"Beware. Something is stalking us," he whispered to the others.

Goran gripped his axe, and Gwendolyn nocked her bow.

With a howl, the demon attacked and raced into their camp. The dwarf was the first one it encountered and with a backhand, it sent the dwarf Goran flying into the undergrowth. It turned for its next attack, and Gwendolyn put arrow after arrow into the creature. It did not flinch.

Celedant saw his dwarf guide flipped head over heels by the attacker and he immediately readied a spell. Lowering his staff he sent a blast of white-hot energy that flowed forth in waves and as each broke upon the attacker, Celedant heard his howls of pain.

The light that now illuminated the thing showed an odd-looking man, and this puzzled Celedant. Then his mind registered the fact that he had seen such beings described in some ancient texts he had studied. It was a demon.

As this realization hit him, Azimuth simultaneously shouted out, "Demon!"

Drawing his sword, Azimuth charged forward and struck the demon twice before the creature uttered a word that threw him backward against the trunk of a tree.

Celedant lowered and aimed his staff once again and sent a bolt of energy at the creature which struck the demon in its side and threw it back to its right. Before Celedant could strike again, Goran approached the dark figure from behind and struck it with his axe. The weapon hit the demon between its shoulder blades and stuck.

Enth felt the blinding pain and knew it was bleeding dark blood from the wizard's spells and from the arrows that kept stabbing him like needles in a pin cushion. Despite its pain, Enth backhanded the dwarf once again and sent him rolling across camp.

With the axe still embedded in its back, the demon looked for the wizard, now clearly visible in the light of the full moon. Celedant cast another spell and a wave of pure white light washed over their enemy. The illumination reacted with its skin and peeled away layer after layer as Enth struggled to advance.

Goran pounced on the demon's back and plunged his dagger in and out of Enth's neck. The dagger ripped into its neck unceasingly and Enth could feel its life force flowing out of its body.

Gwendolyn raced up to Enth and put an arrow through one of its eyes. Slowly, its form began to disintegrate and ooze down into the ground.

Suddenly Goran was no longer hanging onto the creature's back. Enth had disappeared into thin air, leaving behind a pile of dark ash.

The dwarf fell to the ground in surprise and looked at Celedant.

"That was a right tussle. What was that foul beast?"

"Some sort of demon," the wizard replied. "One I believe that was on a mission to eliminate us."

Goran smilingly wiped blood from his face. "Well, that was a fight to be remembered."

Celedant motioned to the dwarf. "Come, let's see to your wounds."

Many miles away, Melgor felt the bond between the demon and himself tear in two and fade. Searing pain ripped through his head and he screamed, but not just because of the pain. The warlock knew at once that Enth had failed in his attempt.

Melgor nursed the pain in his head, threw up his hands and shouted, "Incompetent demon!"

He realized that it would take time before he was able to build up enough strength again to call forth another monster from the pit. There was little else he could do now but wait, He'd strike again as soon as he was able.

As Halsbred rode ahead of the four travelers as they again continued south, he found a perfect place to trap them and end his journey.

The following day he set ten mercenaries ahead to ambush the dwarf, the two elves, and Celedant. They lay in wait at a roughly hewn wooden bridge covered in lichen in the depths of the forest.

Surrounded by the idyllic scene of evergreens and moss-covered terrain, the four companions crossed the bridge and when they reached the middle, the mercenaries attacked, five from each direction.

"I'll take the ones in front," Goran called. "Guard me back."

Azimuth drew his sword and Celedant began chanting a spell. Goran and his double-bladed axe met the attackers and he deftly disarmed the first mercenary and shouldered him over the bridge's railing to splash in the swiftly flowing river. Gwendolyn jumped up on the railing as only her elven heritage could allow and she began peppering the mercenaries with arrows.

Goran slammed the head of his axe into the pit of the stomach of a second mercenary and then finished him off with a quick blow to the back of his head. He doubled over and fell.

Celedant's spell had slammed into the first three attackers from the rear, stunning them and knocking them to the rough-hewed planking of the bridge. The following two vaulted their fallen comrades, only to face Azimuth.

The first quickly fell under Azimuth's blade. The second showed a skill that almost matched the dragon's until an arrow struck the man in his heart.

Celedant cast a second spell at the three men he had knocked down earlier and sent small spheres of energy at the fighters. The first three bursts slammed into one man and hurtled him backward. Only the bridge's railing kept him from falling into the ice-cold water and he slowly got to his feet and limped off into the forest.

Gwendolyn sighted the wounded man with her bow, but decided to let him live. He would later die of his wounds in the deep forest.

Goran was having a grand time and laughing while he dealt with the last three attackers. His laughter so disturbed the attackers as Goran waded into them that his axe moved magically through their defensives with no resistance. Soon one fell and then another to the dwarf's axe. The final attacker turned and ran, soon disappearing into the thick forest.

Goran cleaned his axe on the shirt of one of the dead and swiftly searched the body. He came away with the gold pieces Halsbred had paid the men.

Goran held up the shiny loot.

"Why would men with gold in their pockets attack us?"

Azimuth smiled. "Because they wanted more."

The dwarf searched the others and pocketed their gold as well.

"Let's hope that's the reason," Celedant said, "but all the men had the same amount of gold with the same markings. That strikes me as strange. First a demon, and now this. We must look to our safety even more from here on out."

The company dumped the bodies in the river, cleared the bridge and then continued south, keeping their eyes open for additional traps.

Weeks passed after the ill-fated attack by the mercenaries. Halsbred had learned that Celedant was going to the Stonesplitter Clan, the largest of the dwarvan kingdoms. It had become a well-known fact on Dragon Isle before the warlock's departure.

Knowing this, Halsbred had detoured around that kingdom to find the Keystone clan. They had been at odds with the Stonesplitters for over two hundred years, ever since the Keystone Dwarves had struck a vein of silver in territory the Stonesplitters considered their own.

The dispute had been settled by a gathering of the clans because nothing would have been gained if the two strongest clans had gone to war. Had the clans not been appeased, the incident could have ended in open warfare, and allowed the orcs to settle more comfortably in the valleys and caves of the eastern mountains. It was then the Keystone Dwarves' power that kept the eastern side of the Mordolwyn Mountains less appealing to the orcish raiders.

The mine was then worked by dwarves from other clans and the wealth from it was shared, but this still rankled the clans. They did not like having what they assumed should have been their own wealth spread among their distant kin.

Halsbred now approached the Keystone Dwarves, but not openly. He settled his remaining men in the clan's city and sought out the dregs of dwarven society to gather a motley crew that consisted of all manner of lawbreakers, outsiders and castoffs of the clan.

Once they were all assembled, he told them about the Stonesplitters and about a certain man who would be visiting. They could have cared less about the mission. Most of them just wanted the gold the warlock was offering.

In a smoked-filled public room of one dark, dank inn, built for the tall traders who frequented the city, Halsbred met with the leaders of the dwarves he had hired. He lavished food and ale on them before describing the mission. If it bothered them, he did not see it in their eyes. In fact, that they were to kill Celedant's party in the Stonesplitter city hardly phased them. Halsbred knew he had the right dwarves.

Gathering up his ragtag group of mercenaries, Halsbred headed into the forest as far away as possible from the Keystone Clan. The weather was fine, despite the slowly melting snow on the ground. He set up his camp near the south path and waited for Celedant to ride past.

All it would take was for one of the dwarves to point him out, and the warlock's life would be forfeited. Halsbred wondered if he were destined to be both a hunted man himself as well as the hunter of Celedant.

His northmen mercenaries did not seem to mind the snowy forest camp, and Halsbred was content to sit and wait.

CHAPTER ELEVEN

Celedant's party had been traveling several weeks in the foothills of the Mordwelian Mountains when they reached the wide trail that ran west into Stonesplitter territory. Turning onto the wagon-rutted road, they made their way to the clan's holding, a small city surrounded by a well fitted stone wall with stout towers and a gatehouse.

Several dwarves wearing chain mail guarded the road at the gate. Goran spoke briefly with them and a then a black-haired dwarf came forward and spoke for a long while with Goran.

Finally Goran returned and explained the situation to Celedant.

"They said we can enter, but I'm to be responsible for ye three. They are used to traders, but the four of us appearing out of the wild has them unsettled. Come on. The Trader's Inn has been built for taller folk like yerselves."

The dwarf mounted his mountain horse, and they all entered the town.

The houses were made of stone with exquisite workmanship and thatched roofs, but the Trader Inn stood out like a sore thumb. It was built of wood and taller than any of the other buildings around it in an area where several long storehouses had been built.

The four dismounted and several young dwarves led their horses and mules to the stables. The dwarves would have their things sent up to their rooms after they paid.

The inside looked like any other public house around the world. There were tables, benches and mismatched chairs, but beneath the chipped paint, Celedant noticed the excellent craftsmanship that had gone into their creation. The four sat back in chairs around a small table with four tankards of ale in front of them, the foam dripping down the sides.

After several draws, they admitted it was the best they had had in recent memory.

"How do ye plan on getting to talk to the Stonesplitter?" Goran asked.

Celedant brought forth a wrinkled packet.

"I have a letter of introduction from my masters to the Lord Stonesplitter. I'll deliver it in the morning and hope for the best."

Goran laughed. "We'll deliver it together. Most of me kindred canna speak the common tongue. Only the wayward like meself and the traders. Stonesplitter should…but those around him might not. I'll be yer interpreter."

The next morning while they broke their fast Goran reported his findings to others.

"I have discovered that the clan chief lives within the mountain. They have carved out quite a space in there. The problem is that they donna allow anyone other than a dwarf to enter the inner city. I can take the message in, but then we'll have to wait and see what comes of it."

Goran had his best clothes on when they exited the Trader's Inn. Celedant had pressed his own clothes and combed his tangled hair for a possible meeting with the dwarves. Azimuth and Gwendolyn stayed at the inn while the two of them wound their way up the street, drawing stares from the dwarves going about their business. Finally they arrived at the doors that led under the mountain.

The ever-vigilant guards stopped them at the gate.

"Only dwarves can enter. The outsider can wait by the stables in the shade."

Celedant nodded to Goran and silently wishing the dwarf good luck, he made his way to the horse stockade to admire the mountain horses. The wizard drew stares and many suspicious looks as he lounged about the stables.

The guards had recognized the traveling dwarf and let him in immediately. After bidding Celedant goodbye, Goran disappeared into the black maw of the mountain, but not before asking the way to the Stonesplitter section.

"I'll take ye, traveler," a guard replied. "The mine shafts run off in many directions. We wouldna want ye to go down one of those."

Goran thanked the guard and tossed him a coin and the guard quickly led him down several flights of stairs.

When they had reached the proper level, he pointed to the Stonesplitter's area in the habitable portions of the mountains. The doorway was guarded by two dwarves who regarded Goran suspiciously, but he quickly set the two guards at ease. One led him right to the Stonesplitter's chief councilor. Goran thanked his guide and approached the doorway.

The guard by the door called for him to halt. The other, with a smile on his face, asked, "What brings ye to our master's doorway?"

Goran smiled back, trying to put both guards at ease.

"I bring an important letter from the wizards of Dragon Isle."

"I canna let ye in to see Stonesplitter himself, but I can get ye in to see his aide," the smiling door guard said.

The aide to the ruler of the Stonesplitter clan was busy writing at his desk when Goran entered the room. He did not look up, but gruffly said, "Put what ye bear in that pile."

Goran cleared his throat, but did not want to upset the dwarf.

"Tis a letter from the wizards of Dragon Isle."

Goran's announcement made the dwarf stop scratching away at his document and look up.

"Ah, traveler, ye say it's from the Isle? Hand it over and I'll get it to the Stonesplitter right away. Now ye may go."

He took the packet and went back to his writing.

Goran found himself outside in a matter of several clicks of the clock and he went directly back out to Celedant, enjoying the sunshine.

"Tis done," the dwarf told him. "It be delivered. Now we must wait and see when the aide gets around to showing it to the Stonesplitter."

CHAPTER TWELVE

After enjoying a few drinks at what was now Goran's favorite pub, Celedant and his friends were walking up a cobblestone street after sunset. Suddenly, from a side alley a dozen dwarves, all armed to the teeth, rumbled out of the darkness.

Goran had his axe out in an instance and cut down the first two attackers. Turning around, he was then kept busy parrying the other two swords with his axe.

Celedant had been startled at first, but his training, drilled into him for years, immediately took over. Had he been alone in that moment of hesitation, the assassins would have killed him.

Now he attacked. He slowed his breathing as he drew his sword and began casting a spell. At the same time he caught a dwarf's axe on his own blade and deflected it downward. His spell, a relatively simple one, then shot forth from his hand and sent a small orb that hit the chest of one of the attacking dwarves. Electricity fanned out from the impact and brought the dwarf to a halt and he began to shake from the energy dispersing through his body.

In an instant he fell over backward, unconscious in the street.

Meanwhile Gwendolyn had her bow out and was shooting arrow upon arrow into the attackers. Celedant was still busy with another attacker. He deflected the first blow and as his axe struck sparks on the stone road, Azimuth arrived and brought the pommel of his sword down, clouting the dwarf on the head and knocking him out.

Another two dwarves appeared behind them, one with a small sword and a dirk in his hands and he rushed the wizard. Goran spun his axe around and took down one of the opponents by plunging his axe into his attacker's face. Seeing the other fall, the second one raced away.

Celedant's foe had no such inclination, though, and he swung back and forth at the wizard. The wizard went down on one knee under the onslaught from the powerful dwarf. Then Goran used the side of his axe to bash in the dwarf's helmeted head and knock him out. He tumbled in a heap onto the cobble stones.

By the time it was all over, the street was crowded with torch bearing dwarves, and the city watch circled the dead and tied up those who were unconscious.

The watch captain was very apologetic and claimed that they would get to the bottom of this and declared that whoever had sent these rascals would be caught and hung.

The next day a message arrived for Goran that the clan leader would meet with them. They all felt that last night's escapades were the real reason for the message, rather than the letter of introduction itself.

Gilbert, the clan chief, had been willing to wait a year before having the wizard brought before him, but now that same annoying wizard, Celedant, had been attacked in Stonesplitters' city. Out of fear of retribution from Dragon's Isle, the chief was now forced to see the young man.

Gilbert received them in a low-ceilinged hall crammed with thirty or more dwarves. He sat, resplendent in his bright blue clothes, in a high back chair at the end of the hall. His bushy black beard spilled down past his belt and into his lap unplaited and gleaming in the lamp lit hall.

Goran, Celedant and the two elves made their way to the clan chief and bowed low.

He looked them over disdainfully.

"Why are ye here?" he asked bluntly. "I know Goran, the traveler, but not these Islanders."

Gilbert's reference to Celedant being an Islander and not a wizard of Dragon Isle rankled Celedant, but he stood tall before Gilbert as he spoke.

"I bring a message of peace from the elders of Dragon Isle, yet all I get in return is bloodshed in the streets."

Goran winced. Normally, no one would dare speak to the chief in this manner. Goran feared the outcome from that, but Gilbert merely nodded.

"A most unfortunate occurrence, and one that will be attended to. All the attackers were dwarves from the Keystone Clan. Rest assured. They will answer to me."

Celedant smiled. "My lord let them answer to me and to Dragon Isle, not to you. Like I said, I come with a message of peace."

Gilbert's face now turned red with rage to be so spoken to in such a way again.

Even more frightened now, Goran took a step back from Celedant as the wizard continued.

"I have come to offer mediation. It is imperative that the dwarves set aside their age old differences and unite in the coming days. Already our scouts have discovered a massive orc build-up in the western Mordolwyn Mountains. They intend to attack steading after steading here and destroy and pillage your people. They are many thousand strong."

The wizard's words brought a muttering of frightened awe throughout the hall. The Stonecutter clan was the largest, Gilbert knew, but it could only muster some six hundred warriors. That was enough for the occasional orc incursion, but now, with that many orcs gathered? How could they fight them off?

Gilbert knew the wizard was right.

Celedant continued. "You must be the power that unites the clans to go forth to battle. It is the only way, and you are the only one capable of such a monumental task. I entreat you to reach out to the Keystone Clan and to the others to side with you in the coming crisis."

The flattery Celedant had included to stroke the dwarvan chief's ego worked.

A message both conciliatory and stern concerning Celedant's recent unprovoked assault was sent by Gilbert — who still considered himself the affronted party in the two clans' dispute — to the Keystone Chief inviting him to attend him at his court.

Basset, the Keystone clan chief, quickly responded with a return message. He offered Gilbert the sincerest apology and assured him that they would root out the leaders behind such an act. More importantly, agreed to attend a meeting with the Stonesplitter.

A week passed before a runner came to Gilbert's great hall with word that a party of twenty Keystone Dwarves, led by Basset, with a ginger beard and bald pate, were waiting at the gate. Gilbert immediately summoned Celedant, Azimuth, Goran and Gwendolyn to be ready and he personally went down to the gatehouse.

The Keystone Dwarves were waiting patiently at the open gate as Gilbert appeared with only his scribe and two bodyguards, his less than subtle way of announcing that he did not fear the Keystone Dwarves.

The two chiefs walked up to each other and hugged, as was customary, and spoke a little before winding their way back toward the great hall. Dwarves and non-dwarves had lined the street for this odd event and stood in silence as the two chiefs disappeared into the great hall.

Basset was of course wary, as were his soldiers and scribes, but all they saw was Gilbert's curiosity, not malice, directed at the Keystone company. He saw that this hall was not much different than his own, in fact. except that the ceiling was lower, but he knew of the riches that lay below the floors, even though it seemed that little of that wealth had been spent on these living and working quarters. Still, he was sure that the dwarves were busy right now directly beneath Basset's feet.

Gilbert sat down in his high-backed chair and motioned Basset to a similar chair at his right and after Basset sat, Gilbert turned slightly inward to allow two of them to speak more directly.

Gilbert's man servant then clapped the butt of his spear on the stone and announced, "Let the meeting commence."

Gilbert waited for the Keystone Chief to speak first.

Basset began. "I must apologize to both the Stonesplitter Clan and Dragon Isle for the attack of recent." He nodded at the tall figure of Celedant, whose head nearly bumped the ceiling.

"The wizards of Dragon Isle take no grievance for the aforementioned action," Celedant said quickly.

"It is not so for the Stonesplitters," Gilbert interrupted. "Our city has been penetrated and our guests attacked." He slammed his fist on his chair's arm rest.

Basset, a stern look now on his face, said, "I think that me being here shows the horror we all feel."

Celedant interrupted them both before things could get out of control.

"This incident is best put aside," he said, "due to the more pressing news that I bear. I have informed Chief Gilbert that orcs are massing for an invasion into the east. If we can't form an alliance, all of your steadings will be crushed, one after another."

This caused a great stir among the dwarves who, as yet, had not officially been told of the imminent attack. That was to Celedant's liking as it made evident it was a perfect time for all to have these two most powerful clans together in one place.

Basset looked to Gilbert. "Is this true?"

The other dwarf grimly nodded. "The wizards of Dragon Isle say it is so, and I believe them. A gathering of the clans has never occurred, but in light of the information Celedant has brought us, I see no other way but to join forces to combat the oncoming horde."

Basset inclined his head forward. "I also trust what Dragon Isle says."

Goran inched timidly forward until Gilbert became aware of him.

"What troubled news do you bring, traveler?" he asked Goran.

Goran motioned to the wizard. "Before I met and brought Celedant here, I was in the west and I caught several lone orcs messengers. I was able to get information out of them...before I dispatched them. They said they were traveling the mountains and plains looking for tribes to join the coming venture. From what they told me, I believe they will come in the spring, when the mountain passes begin to melt. We have until then to gather as many warriors as possible and stop them in the passes. Their numbers will be a hindrance in those narrow canyons."

Gilbert nodded his head. "Yer tactics are wise, and we appreciate yer information. Now it seems that we must do the impossible and unite the clans. It has never been done before. What say you, Basset? Will yer warriors go to battle with us?"

The other chief knew he could not appear cowardly in front of the gathered dwarves. Nor could he dismiss the claims of a Dragon Isle wizard or of a traveler with the fame of Goran.

"Me clan will go to war, but who will lead?" he asked. "That is the key sticking point. In modesty, I admit I have no head for tactics and war. I am, and always will be, a miner at heart. The other clans may not see it so black and white, though. We have but five hundred warriors among us, including the untrained. With the addition of five clans, we can double that number, but I fear they will not subject themselves to yer command as easily as I have, Gilbert. Even though I am fine with your leadership, there will be dwarves in my clan who won't easily accept this. I might have to use a bit of force to show them the light. It would be better if they heard our purpose from Celedant and Goran. The latter is well known and, as you know, much respected among all the clans."

Gilbert acknowledged Basset with another nod of his head. "We also must send delegates to show our mutual support. The others may doubt the severity of the threat if they don't see that our clans are working together, especially since our problems together in the past are so well noted."

"It might behoove us to have the backing of the Theirrian clerics on this mission," Basset said. "The steadings will more likely heed a call to arms with the warrior clerics on our side. We can send Celedant to the abbot Bazak with a letter from both our clans. That might persuade him to join our cause."

"Now that is an excellent idea," Gilbert agreed.

The next morning, a letter from the dwarvan chieftains in his possession, Goran took the lead, and the four adventurers headed west deeper into the mountains.

They followed a small rough path up into the snowcapped peaks of the Mordolwyn range. Celedant's horse shied away from the precarious edge, above a thousand-foot drop. The wind was freezing and cut through their clothes in giant gusts. The wizard was uneasy, but his companions were calm and they chatted back and forth, turning their bodies to sign with Gwendolyn.

Seeing Celedant's nervousness, Azimuth spoke to him telepathically. *Don't worry, my friend. Should you slip and fall, I will change back into a dragon and catch you.*

That is reassuring, Celedant replied telepathically. *Thank you.*

Soon the mountains opened up and ahead of the four companions rose a single mountain standing alone amidst the surrounding peaks.

Goran, who was leading, pointed and called out to the others.

"Mount Thierry, home of the mighty warrior clerics."

They continued their precarious ride, ducking under a cascading waterfall, the stone path now slippery with water and the mist settling on their clothing. As they emerged, they came face to face with a stone wall built across the narrow path.

A dwarvan head appeared at the top of the five rod- structure and called out.

"Why are ye on this trail?"

Goran, still in the lead, replied loudly so he could be heard over the waterfall.

"We are emissaries for the chief of the Stonesplitter clan, the mighty Gilbert. We bear important papers for Abbot Bazak."

Suddenly a hidden door opened in the middle of the wall and a heavily armed and armored dwarf advanced toward them. He wore a bear cloak and underneath they could see a complete suit of chain mail with added steel reinforcements. The dwarf cleric carried a double headed axe and had two maces tucked into his belt. He approached Goran.

"Show me the seal of Gilbert," he said. "I served the Stonesplitter years ago."

Celedant passed the letter forward. The cleric took a look at it and motioned them to pass.

"Keep to the left of the path and ye'll find our monastery."

The party pushed onward and as they took the left-hand pass, they saw the monastery in the distance on an open space at the bottom of a mesa. Portions of its walls hung over a thousand-foot drop-off, and the structure, built right against the walls of the up-jutting mesa, looked to be at least six levels high,.

They rode to a stout wooden gate and, after being questioned, were told where to find the abbot's quarters. Once there the four of them would first need to convince the under abbot of their need to speak with Bazak.

As Celedant, Goran, Azimuth and Gwendolyn entered the massive facility, they were astonished by what they saw. To the left of a cobbled road more than fifty clerics, dressed in full armor, were training with their weapons against upright wooden logs. To the right were the stabled mountain horses. Nearby several blacksmiths worked diligently at their anvils.

They passed through another gate, where the cobbled road ended, and two young novices hurried forward to take their horses to the stables.

"Ye'll find the assistant abbot just inside that door," one novice told them,

The company dismounted and walked toward the door.

"This is not a monastery, but a citadel," Azimuth said, impressed. "Even the doors to the buildings are reinforced with iron."

As they climbed the stairs, Goran filled them in. "Thierry is the patron god of warriors and thus his servants must be ready for battle at all times. That is why we are here. If we have the backing of Thierry's clerics, it will lend credence to our cause."

"What have you heard about the abbot? Will he be likely to support us?" Celedant asked.

"I have never met him or been here. I have only met some of the brothers on their journeys to different steadings," Goran replied. "They have been more than happy to step in and defend any dwarf in need of help. Frankly, these clerics walk a fine line between being bloodthirsty warriors and gentle religious followers. Abbot Bazak is a warrior at heart and he will see the wisdom in Chief Gilbert's letter and in our mission."

They entered the building and saw three doors ahead of them. The middle one was open, and a meticulously dressed dwarf sat behind a well-ordered desk. He had on a habit, not armor, the first sign the companions had that this was actually a monastery. He had a carefully tonsured haircut and thick, bushy mustache that hung down to his chest.

Goran and Celedant stood in front of him and waited for the dwarf to look up from the parchment he was reading.

When he did, he said, "Well...you're a good reason to put a stop to reading endless inventories. Me name is Tisic. Tell me. What mysteries do ye bring?"

Goran stepped forward. "I am Goran the traveler. This is the wizard Celedant and Azimuth from the Dragon Isle and Gwendolyn, me ward. We have a letter of introduction from Chiefs Gilbert and Basset."

Celedant handed the letter to Tisic and stepped back as the cleric opened it and read through the introduction.

"Well," he said, "the chiefs — who usually can't abide each other, we know — seem united in their trust of ye. I'll take this to Bazak. Ye can wait in me office."

It took thirty clicks of the clock for the dwarf to return, but he had a smile on his face and he motioned for them to follow him.

"Bazak seems interested in what ye have to say. The missive has him perplexed."

They wound their way through a labyrinth of passages until Tisic opened a thick wooden door that led into a garden. There, sitting on the edge of a fountain, was the abbot.

Bazak was a thin dwarf, but wore his armor with ease. His sword's scabbard looked well used, as did the giant war hammer that hung from his belt. The hammer head was a block of granite mounted on an intricately carved wooden handle.

Tisic made the introductions and backed out of the garden, shutting Celedant and the others in with the abbot. Bazak held the letter in his hand and introduced himself.

"An odd letter that interests me greatly," he said to his visitors. "These two clans are enemies. Yet something has brought them together."

"There is a dire situation arising in the south," the wizard replied. "This document might explain it. Stonesplitter, himself, trusted us with it." Celedant handed the dwarf a second parchment.

It took Bazak more time to read and then reread it before he looked up with a stern look.

"Traveler, ye are well known to us here. Ye saw this for yerself?"

Goran looked the abbot straight in the eye.

"On me journey, I caught several orcs and goblins heading for what will soon be a large gathering of immense proportions. All bore the same message. They were to come together at the base of the mountain passages…and be ready for war."

The abbot looked to Celedant. "What say the Masters of Dragon Isle?"

The wizard straightened up and responded. "It would be a sore blow against the orcs to have the dwarvan nations all in one accord. We have persuaded Gilbert and Basset to join forces, but we still need dwarves from the other steadings to gather an army that would be large enough to stop the invasion. Without their help, there will be no stopping the orcs and their allies."

Bazak looked to Goran. "What are yer plans?"

"We are going town by town to gather as many warriors as possible before the spring thaw begins," Goran explained. "Once we know what pass they will be using, we can set up defenses and be ready to stem the tide."

The wise abbot nodded. "I will send a dozen of my senior clerics to accompany ye. The dwarves might react better if they know that I myself will lead me Therians to war."

The four smiled. This was better than they had hoped. Not only would Bazak aid in their diplomatic mission, he would even send his clerics into battle.

"Besides," the abbot added, "we will have a wizard with us, yes? That's got to count for something."

Celedant's mind was awhirl. First Gilbert and then Bassett and now the head of the Therians thought he was some god-sent savior. The wizard knew he was but freshly released from the isle and that he had limited experience fighting. Standing there with these fierce cleric dwarves, he felt self-doubt and, frankly, had become uncertain of the whole situation.

Goran slapped Celedant on the back.

"I have seen Celedant in action against a demon," he boasted. "His bravery and spells saved the day."

At the mention of the demon, Bazak reached up to touch his war hammer necklace.

"We will need such stout-hearted strength in what is to come."

Thus began Celedant's travels throughout the Mordolwyn Mountains.

He visited clan after clan, from the smallest that consisted of forty odd members to the largest with several hundred. Along with the wizard, Gilbert's and Basset's emissaries and the Thierrian clerics did their best to persuade the clans of the value of their joining forces, particularly against a orcan invasion.

Goran, now the renowned traveler, added his own strength to the others' warning. Until now, Celedant had been unaware that his traveling companion was such a widely well-respected dwarf.

When asked, himself, Goran merely shrugged.

"I don't like notoriety," he'd say. "That's why I travel so much. I prefer the road to the adulation. I bring news of the outside world and sometimes accompany caravans to the east or north. I especially like to look after the smaller clans. They can so easily be destroyed by a sizable orc host. They will fight just because I am here, though they will not send many. They will follow Gilbert, too. He was a renowned fighter before becoming clan chief upon his father's passing. I suspect we will gain more than a thousand warriors from these smaller steadings.

"The eastern dwarves will not readily accept the notion and might be downright hostile," he warned Celedant and the others. "They keep to themselves and will not care much about what happens in the west. We will be outnumbered, but when riled, dwarves are protective of their lands and can be quite a force to reckon with. Besides, we'll have ye along. And, as Bazak said, that's got to count for something."

Only then did the wizard fully realize that he himself was going to be counted on for the oncoming battle. With a shocked face, he turned toward Azimuth for help, but wasn't sure what he should say.

"I am ready to follow you wherever the road takes us," the dragon assured him. "Even into battle if necessary."

Celedant turned a little green, and Goran laughed.

"The old ones didna tell ye of that possibility, did they? Ha, donna worry. I will be beside ye too, and I will not die by an orc's hand. That I assure ye."

"But what about me?" Celedant asked with a plea in his voice. "I'm much taller than you and will be a fine target for any orc archer."

"Learn to duck," Goran said with a smile. Gwendolyn began signing and Goran translated. "She'll follow, too. Having a wizard will be good luck."

Celedant, with Goran's help, had started learning to sign with Gwendolyn. He could pick up a few words she said, but he was still unsure of his own hand gestures. He signed back what he thought was "thank you" and both Goran and Gwendolyn laughed.

"Ye just wished her horse a good time," the dwarf explained.

The four of them continued with their travels among the steadings. Despite having the support of both Stonesplitter and Keystone, they still ran up against towns and mining camps that promised no help at all. As Goran had pointed out, though, they would probably send small parties once they accepted the news.

Melgor had been waiting and resting to regain his strength until he heard the rumors that Celedant was traveling through the Mordolwyn Mountains.

He began drawing the runes for his ritual to cast the summoning spell. Soon the same vortex appeared over the detailed drawings on the floor. This time he called forth a force stronger than the last arrogant demon. Deep from the pits of the nine hells he called forth not one, but four hellhounds.

The vortex swirled and out of it came four massive, dog-shaped monsters.

They stood in front of him, man-sized, with mottled, swirling red coats of fur. It looked like lava flowed in their veins. Their muzzles were massive, and gleaming white teeth filled their mouths.

The hellhounds stood expectantly in the circle, waiting for Melgor's command, their red eyes boring into the warlock. Melgor chanted a spell and Celedant's opaque figure appeared in the room. The hounds nodded in unison, sniffing the air. Supernatural creatures, they had picked up the scent of the wizard.

Melgor pointed to the figure, and the dogs howled eagerly. Releasing his holding spell on the hounds, Melgor then held the door open for them. They raced out of the room in silence, intent on picking up and following the wizard's trail.

Celedant and his growing band of warriors continued traveling from clan to clan trying to get support for the oncoming war. He now traveled with his regular companions, a dozen Therians and clerics from the Stonesplitter and Keystone clans, all of whom he got along with nicely.

One afternoon he and his companions entered the small village of the clan Silvervein. Theirs was a simple village, located in the deep mountains and boasting a population of no more than a hundred dwarves. It was a quaint place with small stone and turf houses. Their ancestors had stumbled upon a silver lode there, and that was how they got their name. Now, since the vein had run dry, the dwarves were shepherds and stonemasons.

One small inn catered to the locals and to the occasional visitor. It was now full of the coming and goings of these strangers along with the many the clerics who traveled with Celedant.

News seldom came to the remote clan, and notice that there was going to be a war weighed heavily on all the members. Celedant and his companions sat down at a table eating and drinking with some of the local dwarves while the clerics discussed the coming war with the clan elders.

Suddenly like a howl from the depths of the abandoned mine pit echoed throughout the village. All talking stopped. Goran stood up, axe in hand.

"That's no wolf," he told his companions. "Come with me."

He made his way through the hushed crowd and out into the snow-covered street. The white flakes were falling left to right as he readied his axe and, following his lead, Celedant and Azimuth prepared for battle. Gwendolyn had her bow out and an arrow already notched.

The first howl was answered by several more, and the clerics and several warriors of the clan rushed out into the street from the little inn and took defensive positions. The howls drew nearer and nearer to the village. Azimuth, Goran, Gwendolyn, Celedant and the dwarves all stood ready, as four dog-like creatures from the depths of any of their worst nightmares made their way up the street. The creature's maws flamed red and they drooled what appeared to be steaming blood down onto the roadway, melting the snow as they came forward.

Their muscular shoulders were higher than any dwarf, but Goran advanced to meet them straight away. He pushed one aside, setting its cloak afire, and swung his axe into another. The creature howled in pain as the axe cut deep into its chest. The other creatures had now picked up the wizard's scent and rushed past Goran and into the crowd of warriors and clerics in the street. Gwendolyn fired arrow after arrow into one beast, but each shaft caught fire upon impact.

One of the dog-like creatures was upon Celedant before he could call forth his spell. He held up his staff, and the monster bit down on it. The wizard pushed the monster off to arm's length as it gnawed on the wood, its bright white teeth and bloody mouth trying desperately to reach him. He strained against the monster's weight while calling forth a spell of pure energy and channeling it through his staff. The rod blazed white-hot, lighting up the sky, and the hellhound disappeared in a loud explosion of blackness.

Meanwhile, two clerics cornered another beast. One held the monster at bay with her shield and mace while the other cast a spell to hold the monster in place. The hellhound's body jerked as it strained to break the binding spell, but the beast was stilled and the village warriors quickly attacked. Their blades bit into the monster repeatedly until it too vanished in a cloud of black smoke.

Azimuth drew his sword as the monsters rushed the gathering of clerics and warriors. One beast brushed aside several dwarves as if they were not there, and attacked Azimuth. He swung his sword in an arch to slow down the beast and then, switching his arm's momentum, he stabbed it in the face. All the while, arrows thumped into the creature's side. Azimuth's blade went past the red molten face and deep into its shoulder.

The hellhound howled in pain, but attacked back, its maw snapping at Azimuth and making the dragon wish he could change forms right now. Even in his wolf persona, he would have been as large as the hellhounds were. He knew he could not make the change. That could expose his true nature to the dwarves, who were unaware of the existence of a true dragons.

Instead, he ducked, almost losing his footing in the snow, as the hostile creature's teeth snapped the air where his head had been. Stabbing upward into the monster's chest, Azimuth's blade sank to the hilt of the sword and exited the monster's other side. The beast reared up, howling into the night air.

Azimuth's sword and glove began to smolder as Azimuth pulled his blade free and when the beast came down to the ground, Azimuth struck it another blow. This time, however, the hellhound's paw hit Azimuth's leg and knocked him down onto the street, bloodying his forehead when it hit the cobblestones.

One of the dwarves from the village bravely attacked the creature and saved Azimuth from its next, potentially fatal blow. The dwarf was then bowled over by the monster and its teeth ripped through the dwarf's throat.

Azimuth had now recovered, and as the beast attacked another dwarven warrior, he struck from the side with his sword and sliced through the creature's ribcage and into its dark heart. The beast finished savaging one last dwarf, but then blinked from existence, leaving a pile of ash on the street.

Goran was still locked in combat with the first hellhound and found himself being forced toward Celedant by the beast. Goran's mind registered that danger even as he swung his axe repeatedly and the beast stopped to snap and paw at him. Goran was batted around by the monster and his helmet flew off and several rings of his armor were ripped.

The monster finally stood abreast of Goran, held back only by the fierce dwarf's axe blade. Several local dwarves came to Goran's aid and attacked, but they were easily brushed aside by the hellhound. Goran grasped the head of his axe and continued forcing the blade into the monster's mouth, deeper and deeper, and it sliced the beast's jaws. One of Gwendolyn's arrows suddenly pierced the creature's eye, but the beast took no notice of it.

Celedant finished off the beast that had attacked him and turned in time to see Goran knocked to the street by the monster. Celedant called on his wizard power and quickly cast a spell. Small, ice like darts arched out from his hand to impact the monster and cool its fiery interior wherever it struck. The hound reared back, freeing the blade of Celedant's dwarf friend, and Goran quickly surged to his feet and struck the beast's leg, now flailing in the air. His axe bit deep and severed the limb. The hellhound once again howled in deep pain while his severed leg splattered searing hot blood on the white snow until the limb only steamed in the coldness.

The beast sprung up and landed on its remaining front leg. Its large bloody eye looked past the dwarf at Celedant. Blood now dripped from its leg and its mouth as it tried to leap past Goran, determined to accomplish the deed it had been sent to do. The dwarf stood his ground and his axe sang through the frigid air as he brought his weapon down on the crown of the hellhound's head with one, thunderous blow. The creature collapsed in the street.

Goran's bloody axe remained wedged in the creature's skull even as the hellhound continued to push forward toward the wizard. For one moment it was pushing heavily against Goran, and then it was gone.

Celedant stood looking at the bloodied street and in the air above it the foggy breath of the warriors and the clerics, all standing together now. He listened for a moment to the eeriness of the mountain's snowy silence around him.

In all, two of the villagers had been killed. The dwarves took them off to the mortuary, a plain, unadorned house where a callow old dwarf saw to the bodies. The rest went back into the inn.

The inn's proprietor considered the situation and offered a free mug for everyone. Having seen first-hand what their enemy was capable of, the local clan leader readily promised his soldiers their chance for revenge in the upcoming war.

Celedant puzzled over where these demons were coming from. He still had no idea that it had been Melgor sending the summoned creatures to attack him. He was sure, though, that orcs were incapable of such a deed. But who was capable of it…and why was he—or she - so hell bent on destroying him?

CHAPTER THIRTEEN

S everal days had passed before Halsbred learned of the botched attempt on Celedant's life through a message that had been delivered to the clan chief. An envoy from Dragon Isle had been attacked by dwarves from the Keystone Clan, Halsbred had learned, and immediate inquiries were being made throughout that city. Such an affront could not be tolerated.

Halsbred knew that the wizards had always been allies to the dwarvan clans, but now it was rumored that Basset, the Clan Chief, was going to the Stonesplitter steading. This was an unprecedented act.

Halsbred wondered if he could by accident have started something unheard of...the uniting the dwarvan clans. What would the Zeiglon authorities think, he worried, particularly that bloodthirsty Emperor Zachary. That would be by far the most worrisome effect his mission could produce. He dared not go and support the orcs for, once in their clutches, he would be killed or jailed. There was not a vault of gold in all the land that could persuade him to take such a chance.

He wanted to remain in the shadows for as long as possible and he knew that using lackeys was still his best plan. Gathering his surviving rag tag group of mercenaries, he headed into the forest and traveled as far away as possible from the Keystone Clan.

The weather was fine, except for the slowly melting snow on the ground, and he set up his camp near the path south and waited for Celedant to ride past. All it would take was one of the captured dwarves to point him out, and the warlock's life would be forfeited. The mercenaries did not seem to mind the snowy forest camp, so Halsbred was content to sit and wait.

Halsbred reminded himself again that as soon as he had successfully hunted and killed Celedant, he himself would be a hunted man. He did not confide in the mercenaries what was transpiring because he assumed that they might run as soon as the possibility presented itself.

So, he too sat in the cold, awaiting his target.

Goran had been right. Despite the dispatches from both Gilbert Stonesplitter and Bazak, the abbot of the Thierry Order, the eastern dwarves had refused to aid them in their cause as a Confederation of Clans, as the united dwarves had now begun to call themselves. The eastern dwarves remained independent and unwilling to take orders from the Mordwelian dwarves, and they insisted that they would take care of the orcs themselves, should they venture onto their lands.

Well, Celedant thought, one of my jobs is done, oddly enough with an orcan army playing a big role. The dwarves, or at least the majority of them, have joined together, and the newly formed nation will be a topic of conversation for years to come.

Gilbert's steading was situated closest to the passes that the orcs might use and it now housed the only clan large enough for such a host of dwarves to use as a staging ground. As spring approached, the dwarves had begun trickling in and in no time, there were over two thousand dwarves gathered, all eating the steading's food. Before long the wildlife about the lands became scarce.

To ease the burden on his steading, Gilbert decided it was best to approach nearer to the passes and camp close to them. Once they settled in at the main pass, the dwarves began building their defensive positions. Since the orcs could use one or both of the smaller passes to flank the dwarvan army, two fortifications were constructed. The strongest faced the main pass. A smaller wall of forts was built to the rear and they were then interconnected with each other by trenches and walls.

Goran, along with Gwendolyn and several scouts, were sent forward to see if they could get a better feel for when the attack would come and from which direction. They found the orcs easily enough. They were such a blight upon the land that the dwarven scouts could smell the encampment from miles away. The scouts moved carefully to avoid the orcan patrols out hunting for food. Like the dwarvan army's, their supplies were limited.

The dwarves captured several hunting parties who, under duress, admitted that the largest pass was their intended target.

Soon the orcan army began breaking their camp. As the dwarves watched the tent city come down, the various orcan groups and regiments moved to their appointed areas. Goran decided all their activity did point toward the larger pass, just like the hunting parties they'd killed afterward had said.

Goran estimated the orc numbers to be close to five thousand and he also witnessed some fights breaking out between different groups. Only the presence of one huge, plate-mailed orc, riding an immense black horse, seemed to stem the scuffles between groups. Finally the orcs moved out and marched raggedly toward the pass.

Goran and Gwendolyn sent their other scouts back and waited until the last click of the clock before leaving, once they were certain which way the enemy was headed.

They made it back several days ahead of the orcs only to find that Gilbert and the army had been busy at the pass in their absence. After being alerted by the other scouts, all the defenses had been finished, including wooden stakes placed in front of earthen redoubts and small stone forts scattered across the terrain. The orcs would pay dearly, Goran knew, should they attack these small fortresses.

Goran picked the largest fortification in the middle of the defenses and made his way across the staked area and up a rope ladder that had been lowered to him and Gwendolyn. One dwarf climbed down another rope ladder to take their horses behind the walls.

The ingenious, hard work his kin had been able to display amazed Goran. He had never been one to stay still, and even as a young dwarf, he had set off alone and become a solitary traveler for his kin while they had become master miners and hard workers. Their constructed redoubts, he recognized, showed that hard work was a top priority for these dwarves. They had dug and dug and placed unworked stone in the trenches to make their defenses. The orcs would break upon the walls and their superior numbers would be negated.

Goran sat back and admired Gilbert's plan.

Goran could see Celedant and Azimuth standing by themselves and looking quite out of place in the hustle and bustle of the preparations. He walked over to the wizard.

"What do ye think? Sound walls and stout souls."

"My arrows will kill many orcs today," Gwendolyn signed after having positioned herself very close to the wizard.

Celedant, who was well versed in offensive spells, felt his mind go blank as he watched the upper pass. Goran edged in beside him too and shouldered him in the ribs, snapping the wizard out of his stupor. Goran looked around at the eager dwarves and realized that they were looking up at the wizard from Dragon Isle and feeling certain that he had fought many battles and was a true veteran of such encounters.

Several turns of the clock later, the orcs crested the pass and stopped, in some disorder when they lay their eyes on the dwarvan defense work. Arrows soon arched out of the nearest forts and landed amidst the milling orcs. They scattered in all directions until the big orc crested the pass on his black warhorse.

Gilbert slapped Celedant.

"It begins. See yon fellow on the crest? It would be greatly to our advantage if ye could do something about him."

Celedant looked doggedly at the orc. "I'll see what I can do." He began his incantation as the orcs rushed down from the pass toward the dwarves.

Arrows began flying back and forth between the orcs and dwarves, but the orcish arrows mainly bounced off the thick iron of dwarven armor. Some of the dwarves toppled backward here and there, whenever an arrow found its mark. Lightly armored orcs were felled in great numbers by the skill of the dwarvan archers and crossbowmen. Gwendolyn too sent arrow after arrow at the coming horde.

Celedant released his spell and great columns of fire fell from the sky and enveloped massive swaths of orcs. He then sent fireball spells shooting out of his fort and incinerating many more orcs. The dwarvan clerics also sent spell after spell into the milling enemy.

The great orc in black stood his ground and did not venture forth into the battle. He was able to stay just out of range of the arrows and spells and he dared not offer himself up to the clerics' and wizard's magic.

Soon the first wave of orcs began retreating, even the ones that had engaged the nearest forts, but the large mounted orc would himself still have nothing to do with the battle. He called forth more warriors that pushed or cut their way through the retreating ranks. These orcs were better armored, and the dwarvan arrows had less an effect on them, but the dwarves' crossbows easily penetrated even the best armor the orcs wore.

The new wave of orcs crashed upon the redoubts and crawled up their steep dirt sides and stone walls. dwarvan defenders hurled spears and boulders down upon them and all the while Gwendolyn, with her elven heritage, accurately shot arrow after arrow into the orcs' exposed body parts.

Giant cave ogres came charging with the second wave. These monsters were driven toward the defenses by other orcs wielding long pointed poles pushing them to easily penetrate the redoubts of the dwarves. They pounded against the dry stacked stone forts and the dwarves were swept aside and were forced now to come at the ogres with long pikes and halberds.

The other orcs poured in after the cave ogres and a dire battle ensued. The walls of some forts fell to the pounding and covered the ogres with their dusty debris, but the collapsed structures now left a sloping ramp for the orcs to advance up.

The dwarven bowmen who had been hidden in the interior of the forts now advanced and shot a barrage of arrows into the orcs. The battle hung in the balance until the clerics of Thierry rallied their troops and charged into the fray. They wielded their weapons with mighty blows, and the rest of the dwarves drove into the enemy with a renewed vigor.

Right in front of Celedant the scary head of an ogre appeared, howling in delight at reaching the top of the walls and seeing up close the dwarven flesh that awaited it. Celedant could smell the beast's fetid breath. Goran appeared and shouldered the wizard away and struck him with his axe, hitting the monster in the center of the forehead, the blade settling in deep.

The creature looked cross eyed at the war axe buried in its skull and slowly fell backward. He toppled over the ladder and nearly pulled the traveler's axe with it as he went down.

The orc enemy had gained the parapets in places, but they were quickly cut down by the dwarves. At one of the smaller forts, the orcs gained a foothold and were about to overrun the wall, but the archers in the middle of the fort were at such close range that they easily picked out the orcs' exposed flesh and brought many of them down. Their dwarven comrades formed two-man shield walls and slowly pushed the orcs backward toward the point where they had scaled the wall.

Dwarvan weapons continued to dance through the shields of the orcan warriors and, if one fell, another dwarf took his place. Soon the packed dirt under the inside of wall was filled with bodies as the dwarves slowly pushed back the orcs toward that foothold. When the dwarven shields threatened to fatally trap them against the wall, the orcs began leaping from the earthen height. Some orcs fell outside to be impaled on the spikes the dwarves had embedded in the ground. Ohers fell into the center of the fort and were dispatched quickly by the reserve troops stationed there.

Celedant noticed the enemy captain now drawing closer. The wizard had nearly exhausted his spells in the all-out attack so far, but he had held several powerful ones back in case the tide turned. Under the captain's now close supervision the battle began to sway toward the orcs and their allies.

Nonetheless Gilbert, standing next to the wizard, was in a gleeful mood. Never had he stood against such a foe, and he was elated in the moment. Meanwhile Goran and Azimuth methodically dispatched orc after orc as they climbed up the ramparts. Gwendolyn, having run out of arrows, stood ready with her short sword.

Azimuth swore inwardly at having to keep his true identity a secret. Had he been allowed to change into dragon form, he knew he would have been able to sweep overhead and bathe the attacker in rivers of flame.

Soon several of the smaller earthen redoubts had fallen to the massed attack, and the dwarves there were in dire straits.

The orc commander followed too closely to the third wave of orcs and was now in range of the wizard. Celedant began another spell, sending from his staff a great arc of lightning which threaded through the attacking waves in front of the commander, frying orcs left and right, until it struck the ground thirty paces in front of the captain.

The huge orc smiled, but it was his last moment of joy because the wizard's lightning bolt ricocheted off the stony ground and flew right into the orc's chest plate. Attracted like a magnet to the metal plate mail the orc wore, the lightning struck him squarely in the body and hurled him from his horse to land down on the sandy ground amidst his troops.

He lay on the ground, stunned, and the electricity from the spell popped and sizzled and created a nauseous odor that rose from his charred body inside the oven that his plate mail had become.

The orcs realized that their commander had fallen and they began wilting away. As the news of his demise spread, the entire orc army began retreating back toward the pass.

They were not going to be allowed to go in peace. The dwarves pursued the fleeing orcs and a bloodlust took hold of those defenders who had now turned into the attackers. The dwarves cut into the rear files of the orcs and left a trail of dead bodies behind them as they pursued the rest of the fleeing enemy.

The orcs were being routed, and even their strongest leaders could not persuade the few remaining troops to stand their ground in the face of the bloodied, mad-eyed dwarves charging up the slope after them.

Celedant and Azimuth had no desire to follow the dwarves. Goran shared their sentiment. The dwarf leaned against the parapet, his bloodied war axe propped beside him, his muscles aching from overuse.

Gwendolyn slapped Goran on the back and signed, "Well done."

Celedant, wanting to show off his new mastery of signing, told her, "You did well yourself, Gwendolyn."

She smiled shyly back at him and was secretly happy that he had spared the time to speak to her. Maybe he really was starting to notice her, she hoped.

"Well," Goran interrupted fond gaze passing between Gwendolyn and Celedant, "although the dwarves havena formed one nation yet, it's a start."

Celedant turned to him smiled. "With the treaty signed, I might now be able to return home."

Goran laughed.

"Me friend, we have just begun our travels. If I'm correct, a note to that effect will arrive within the next few days."

CHAPTER FOURTEEN

Melgor could feel the passing of the hellhounds. The agony of their deaths ripped briefly through his body and made him cry out in pain and anger.

He did not realize, though, that they had fallen to a village of dwarves and not to Celedant alone. He was worried. He had attacked Celedant twice using the creatures he'd summoned from the pit, with nothing to show for it. Was Celedant that good? It was possible, but for a newly released wizard and one so young, it seemed highly improbable. Melgor had been powerful himself when he left the academy, but he had been on the Isle for countless years.

At least he had attacked from afar, he thought, and it seemed that Celedant had not been able to follow the origins of the attacks back to him. As much as he hated to admit it, he would have to quit the attacks as they had proven useless. And, eventually, Celedant would figure out who was behind them. After all, the young wizard had been sent to stop Melgor's studies, or so he thought.

Melgor had become so focused on his own needs that he was unaware of the young wizard's true mission.

Taking up a parchment and quill, Melgor began to write his friend Sellis:

Sellis,

Celedant has been loosed after me, and presently is mixed up in some dwarvan business. I will be in hiding for the time being. Should Celedant make an appearance in Partha, I would be delighted, if you could delay him – permanently if possible. I fear he is heading to Zeiglon, as that was where I last spent my time studying. Therefore, he should pass you on his way. I wish you luck and should you succeed in this endeavor, I will pay you a substantial reward.

Melgor

That would get things moving. Sellis was the greediest warlock ever to grace Dragon Isle. Melgor and he had often spoken of their dreams to leave the island and make their way into the world, but that was where their similarities ended. They wanted off Dragon Isle for two completely different purposes. Melgor wanted to continue his studies in demonology. Sellis wanted to amass as much wealth as possible. Just the mention of a reward would have Sellis chomping at the bit to go after Celedant.

Meanwhile, Melgor began packing for his trip west. He would strike out for the capital of the west, Dormin, and stay there until he was forgotten. Once Celedant was disposed of, he would venture back to Zeiglon and pick up where he had left off…studying demonology.

The following weeks were little more than a blur for the young Celedant. He was cheered by all the dwarves for the many spells he had cast, but he felt saddened by all the death he had caused. What choice did he have, though, he asked himself. The orcs were trying to kill him.

The dwarves especially respected him for the spell that had felled the orc general. They now saw what a combined army could do to encroaching enemies and they all signed a new treaty that united them in the face of danger. Gilbert was made their general, should any further danger come.

The usually dour and protective dwarves were offering a great reward for the heroic deeds of Celedant, Azimuth, Gwendolyn and Goran. The humble Celedant declined all such offers, but Goran did take several pouches as "traveling gold."

Goran had been true in his word. Two weeks later, a message arrived.

It read: *Well done. Now, proceed to Partha and evaluate the situation between that country and the Zeiglon Empire.*

There was a celebration prior to the departure of the little group. Gilbert was now the leader of the combined dwarvan armies, and the banquet was held in his huge hall. Plenty of good food and drink was served to all for the going away celebration. The dwarves drank too much, though, and eventually the event turned into a friendly, drunken brawl. Gilbert finally calmed the dwarves down before it got completely out of hand.

Celedant had already excused himself, but Goran stayed through the rest of the raucous gathering. Meanwhile Azimuth had taken a turn about town to watch the night sky and the stars beyond.

Once he had reached an area that was large enough, and out of sight of anyone who might be watching, he transformed and took flight. His heart and mind soared with each powerful down stroke of his wings, and he flew higher and higher into the star-lit sky.

Celedant's voice came through to him telepathically. *What are you doing, my friend?*

Something I have missed for too long, Azimuth replied telepathically. *Too long have I been in the constricting form of an elf. My very being clamored to be free.*

I hope you were careful, my friend. It would create quite a ruckus if the dwarves were to see a full-sized dragon in the skies overhead. Remember, they have only seen your smaller cousins and do not know of your existence, Celedant warned.

Cease your worrying. I am being very careful. Now, if you don't mind, I'm going hunting. I have a hankering for mutton. I spotted a herd a few miles west of here.

Don't take too many. We wouldn't want to anger the local farmers.

I believe I will be satisfied with two fat ones. I'll be back long before morning. No one will even miss me, Azimuth assured his friend.

Gwendolyn had left the party and had waylaid Celedant as he returned to his room. She stood on the tips of her toes and gave him a quick kiss on the cheek.

"What's this?" he signed, giving her a nervous smile that went all the way up to his eyes.

She signed to Celedant. "We won't all be coming back from this. I see it in the stars."

Celedant was concerned about her prediction and made a promise to himself that he would do all he could do to make sure everyone returned, especially Gwendolyn.

He was befuddled by the kiss she had given him. Was it just for good luck or did it mean more?

Either way, he went to his rest with a smile on his lips.

They left for Partha the next day after a rousing thank you from Gilbert and a raucous goodbye from the Stonesplitter dwarves. The inns were still filled with dwarves from the differing steadings and they came out and shouted Celedant's name from the sides of the road and the windows of the homes and businesses along the way.

Goran felt a little off. After spending the past night celebrating with his fellow kin, he wasn't his usual talkative self.

Just to rankle the suffering dwarf, Celedant spent their time on the road regaling him with long tales of Edain and Dragon Isle.

Halsbred needed to know where Celedant was and he sent one of his men to Stonesplitter city to find out. When the emissary reached the gate, he found several dwarves standing around, one with a bandage around his head. They told him that the mighty wizard Celedant had left the day before, heading south.

This was the news that Halsbred had been waiting for. The warlock ordered the camp to be struck, and his men mounted and made ready to leave.

The warlock and his mercenaries rode hard on one of the paths south, but the path showed no sign that their quarry had been down it. The lead mercenary pulled up on his reins and brought his horse to a stop. Halsbred came forward and the soldier pointed out several huge footprints, a sure sign that ogres lived in the area. They dismounted and led their horses on foot, trying to make them remain as silent as possible while they followed the ogre tracks.

Soon they reached the edge of the forest and they caught sight of a huge rock jutting out of a hillside with a significant overhang that was providing shelter to a sizable family of ogres. The adults were over three rods tall and had a manlike appearance, but they were behemoth humanoid creatures, with arms and legs as thick as tree trunks. The men wore mismatched variations of clothes and armor. Their women tended to the fire and children were running about the camp.

The warlock slowly stepped from the tree line and showed himself to the ogres. Once they saw Halsbred, they jumped to their feet and brought up their weapons. The warlock responded by muttering a few words of a spell and a crack of lightning sounded above the ogres before rock rained down on them from where Halsbred's lightning bolt had struck the overhead stone of their shelter.

The largest ogre called out to Halsbred.

"What you want, warlock? We not harmed you or your kin."

"I need a favor and I offer gold in return," Halsbred told him.

That piqued the ogre's interest. Cautiously it asked, "What you want done?"

The remaining ogres spread out, their weapons still held ready as they scanned the trees.

The warlock pretended not to notice or care that the ogres were gathering for a possible attack. He knew his men were well placed and ready to charge on his command.

"A wizard should be passing by soon with a dwarf and two elves as companions. I would have you kill them and keep what you want of their treasure."

Instantly alert, the ogre asked, "They bear treasure?"

"Yes, indeed," Halsbred replied. "They carry treasure, but here is my price." He tossed a heavy sack that clinked loudly when it struck the ground in front of the ogre.

The ogre leaned down, never taking his eyes off the warlock, and grasped the bag, but his huge fingers had difficulty opening the sack and taking a gold piece out. He bit into it and nodded to the others.

"Hmm, good amount of gold," he said. "We kill the ones you want dead."

He turned back to the fire and the other ogres lowered their weapons. Halsbred slowly backed away. He mounted his horse and leading his troop, he quickly raced to the path and turned toward Partha.

Perhaps the ogres would kill Celedant, perhaps not. They would at least slow him down.

Several days later, Celedant and his friends were riding down a meandering trail when they heard a horn off to the west. Goran reined in his horse and called to Celedant.

"That's a signal, or I'm an orc. Come, we must ready ourselves."

The dwarf dismounted and readied his axe. Celedant followed suit by loosening his sword and gripping his staff. Azimuth vaulted off his horse, his sword held ready while Gwendolyn stood on her saddle beneath some solid branches that were hidden under the canopy of the trees.

Goran, Celedant, Gwendolyn and Azimuth reached a small clearing just as five giant ogres burst forth from out of the tree line in front of them. Goran let his reins go and charged the oncoming ogres. Celedant readied a spell and sent small balls of fire from his staff which arced out and struck one of their attackers multiple times, searing its skin where they hit.

That ogre quickly had had enough of the wizard's spell. He rushed back into the forest, thinking that treasure or no treasure, it wasn't worth his life. Then, from out of a nearby tree, an arrow sped toward him and struck the base of his skull. The ogre fell dead.

Closing in on the other creatures, Goran tucked himself into a ball and rolled underneath one of them. His axe lashed out right and left at his target's legs and cut through both its hamstrings. The monster fell screaming.

The remaining two ogres just stood there, confused as to who they should attack, when Azimuth ran at them. Celedant wasted no time either. Using his staff, he sent a lightning bolt at the nearest ogre and it caught the monster in its chest, blasting a huge hole in it. Ogre gore and white ribs exploded into the air and the monster was felled right where he stood.

Goran and Azimuth used the light from the blast of Celedant's lightning to charge another ogre. The dwarf brought up his axe and deflected the monster's great sword to the ground. Its point stuck in the rocky soil, but before the ogre could wrench it free, the dwarf brought his axe down and snapped the sword's blade in two. Goran made the ogre dance out of the way with a backhanded swing while Azimuth stepped forward and sliced two deep cuts in the ogre's stomach. It dropped its blade and grabbed an oversized mace that hung from its belt.

Celedant then cast a summoning spell that brought five wolves into the battle. They attacked the final ogre and kept it occupied while Azimuth closed in on the harried ogre.

Goran was still busy dodging his ogre's mace and striking back with his axe. His blows aimed low and then high at the ogre, but despite his size advantage, the ogre went on the defensive and backed up each time the dwarf struck out. Soon arrows appeared seemingly out of nowhere and darted toward both ogres, but their thick skin kept the missiles from causing any real damage.

The young wizard watched as Azimuth and the wolves battled one of the two remaining ogres. Reacting to the cries of pain from the wounded ogre, the wolves howled and they darted in and out at their target. That ogre managed to kill two of the wolves, and they were only proving more of a hindrance then a danger.

Celedant called again for the power of his staff and he sent out a blast of power that thumped the creature in its left leg. There was an audible crack as the force broke the monster's thigh bone and sent it down on one knee. The wolves redoubled their attacks, and the wizard turned to the other battle where Goran had his ogre trapped.

Goran had driven the ogre backwards and its back was against a tree. It flailed back and forth with the mace, trying to keep the dwarf's axe at bay, and Celedant saw half a dozen deep cuts appear on the beast as Goran pressed the attack. The huge ogre was tiring from fending off the smaller and nimbler dwarf and it suddenly swung its mace too far and unwittingly offered Goran the final opportunity he needed. Leaping forward inside the ogre's reach, the dwarf struck the ogre's chest with his axe, parting the makeshift armor the ogre had been wearing. The war axe sunk deep into the monster and bloody froth formed at the corners of its mouth before it toppled over dead.

Meanwhile Azimuth waited for a chance to strike between the wolves' attacks and wished he could have taken his dragon form, knowing that he could have dispatched both those ogres in no time at all. Celedant looked to the ogre with the broken leg as his spell wore off and the wolves suddenly blinked from existence. All Azimuth did was raise his sword and shout threats before the ogre took off and hopped on its good leg for the tree line. Goran went in to finish off the ogre, but there was no need. An arrow suddenly appeared coming out through its eye.

Goran returned to Celedant, smiling, and covered in his enemy's blood.

"Well done, Celedant, Azimuth, Gwendolyn. Our teamwork continues to improve. Without ye, me and Gwendolyn would have been hard pressed to escape this trap."

Celedant bowed and returned the compliment. "And we most certainly would have fallen to these ogres had the two of you not been here."

"Do you think this was a chance encounter?" Azimuth asked.

"After everything that has already attacked us, I leave nothing to chance," the dwarf replied. "The way they found us, and the signal call, points to a trap. Someone or something wants ye to die before ye reach Partha."

With that ominous thought, they gathered their horses, mounted up and headed south.

Chapter Fifteen

T he small group found the Parthian road and once they reached the foothills, the path turned south. Pushing their horses hard, they eventually exited the hills and gazed upon the vista stretching southward with mile upon mile of forested country.

"This is Northern Partha," Goran told him. "This forest will peter out to grasslands, where the Parthian horsemen rule. This portion of the country is scarcely populated. Come. We're still a week or more from the capital."

They had hardly traveled a mile in this new country when the ground in front of them erupted and sent dirt and rocks high into the sky. Their horses reared, fanning their hoofs in the air and making it hard for the riders to remain seated.

From out of the brush ten mercenaries suddenly charged them, galloping towards their prey. Gwendolyn was thrown from her horse and hit her head on a tree stump. She lay there unconscious, blood pooling about her head.

Goran settled his horse more quickly than the novices Celedant and Azimuth. He rode hard at the attacking riders, followed by Azimuth, while the wizard dismounted and called on the power of the earth and trees. He wanted to rush over to the fallen Gwendolyn, but he knew he had to attack the marauders or all four of them would be at risk of death.

He sent out a lightning bolt that narrowly missed two of the enemy, but the electricity and power of the spell toppled them from their saddles. Their dead bodies hit the forest floor, and their frightened horses scattered.

Goran leaned low into the saddle of his horse as he rode through the line of attackers. Two of the riders swung their swords, missing him and cutting the air just above the dwarf's head, but he deftly swung his axe and caught one of their attackers in the back. He was knocked head over heels off his steed and the man slammed into the ground, never to rise again.

Azimuth charged into the fray as the attackers turned to get to Goran. Before they knew what had hit them, two more attackers fell to the wood elf's longsword. Goran spun his horse in a circle, striking out while parrying the raiders' attacks.

Two of the mercenaries quickly changed direction and took a swipe at Azimuth. The elf nearly lost his seat on his horse, and before he regained control, Celedant had already struck. Another raider rode up to the struggling elf, his sword raised, about to kill Azimuth, when two balls of energy struck him in the chest. As Azimuth righted himself on the horse, he saw that the man was dead in the saddle.

Thank you, my friend, he told Celedant telepathically.

Goran was doing well, considering he was up against four of the raiders. His axe blocked their deadly strokes while he used his horse to ram the flanks of the enemies' horses. Those attackers momentarily lost control of their horses, and the dwarf swung backward and struck one rider down. Fiery bolts of light stuck another as he was just about to run a saber through the dwarf.

The last two attackers took off riding for safety, but Goran swung his axe overhead and let it fly. It struck one rider in the back, pitching him over the head of his mount. Azimuth used his draconic strength to hurl a dagger at the last raider. The dagger flew right past Goran's ear and struck the mercenary in the back of the neck. He remained on his horse for several strides before his now dead body tumbled off and hit the ground.

Goran rode to the others with a big smile on his face.

"Well, that was fun," he said. "But I believe I almost lost an ear there at the end."

Azimuth returned his smile. "There was plenty of space between the dagger and your head. However, it is indeed a wonder I did not hit your head...as it stands out so much."

"Goran, do you still think we fight well together?" Celedant asked the dwarf.

"I said it before and I'll say it again," he replied. "We four make a formidable party." He looked around and his face grew serious. "Gwendolyn!"

He rushed to where the half-elf lay. Seeing the blood all over the back of her head, the dwarf gently eased her up into his lap.

Suddenly Gwendolyn came to and pushed at Goran, signing, "Stop. Stop!"

Celedant reached out his hand to help her up and she stood shakily. Smiling at the tall wizard and aware she probably did not at that moment look her best, she ran her fingers through her hair to dislodge the leaves that were stuck to her bloodied head. Then she pulled a small potion from her pocket and drank it to heal the wound and remove the pain from the blow.

The dwarf quickly bound the wound to keep it from opening back up. He knew head wounds were tricky things.

With everyone now calming down, Goran looked around and spoke.

"First a demon, then men like these, hellhounds, ogres and rogue dwarves, and now base villains. There is too much variance in these attacks. I would say that at least two people are trying to kill us. See here?" He pointed to the dead men on the ground. "These men are carrying the very same gold as the ones who attacked us on the bridge. There must be a warlock riding with them, one powerful enough to cause the trail to rise up and form a wall in front of us."

Celedant, his hand still in Gwendolyn's, drew in a deep breath. "I have been thinking along the same lines, Goran. This is not encouraging."

Half a mile away, Halsbred waited for his brigands to return. His three remaining men were growing more and more nervous as time passed, but he waved them down.

"Be calm. We will wait a bit longer and then go in search of them."

They dismounted and waited a full turn of the clock before mounting up and following in the direction the others had gone. When they reached the site of the battle, Halsbred cast a spell, but he was unable to locate any presence or danger in the area.

This is not good, he thought. Surely his men would have finished off Celedant and the others by now.

It wasn't until they rode out of the heavily forested strand of trees that they saw their comrades, dead and strewn across the brown, needle-covered ground. All bore deadly weapon strikes. Two had obviously been trying to get away when they were killed. Halsbred could feel that magic had recently been used in this place.

One of the mercenaries dismounted and searched the dead. He looked up at Halsbred. "Nothing. They have been picked clean."

Halsbred spoke to his three men in a commanding voice.

"More for the rest of you when the job is done. Come. We must reach Partha before they do."

He turned his horse south, but angled a bit to the east so as not to come upon his quarry.

Goran and the others rode south and encountered several small villages that treated the strangers with suspicion.

"Rarely have I been this far south, so happily my reputation does not precede me," Goran informed Celedant.

A week and a half later, they emerged on the grasslands, and they stopped their horses for a rest as they faced Partha and the sea beyond.

This was the seat of power that Zeiglon so desired, a huge city, protected by stout walls and high stone towers that enclosed the metropolis. It was by far the largest city Celedant had ever seen. It made Edain and Trondheim look like mere villages in comparison.

At the gates they were allowed inside without a by-your-leave.

"We'll find an inn. Then ye can seek out yer contact here in the city," Goran said. "We'll find them…or they will find us. It's only a matter of time." As they rode into the city, he added, "Keep on my heels. We'll find an inn I am familiar with. Shout if yer about to lose me."

With that, he led them through the crowded streets of Partha and took them to a delightful inn. They were well received, and the food was palatable. Over their roast mutton and fresh vegetables, they discussed their next move.

"So, my friend, how are you going to get into the King's court?" Azimuth asked after swallowing a huge bite of his meat. "That is where you can truly judge the tension that exists between Zeiglon and Partha."

"It's best not to mention that country around here," Goran quickly added. "They might think we're from there."

"Good advice," Celedant said. "The letter said to seek out the king's chancellor, or we would be summoned once it is known that we are in the city. He can get us into the halls. Befriending the chancellor will be important because he will know most of what is going on in the country."

Sellis received the message a few weeks after Melgor had penned it. He already knew about the great battle in the mountains where an orc host had been driven away by the combined dwarvan clans, but Melgor's missive mentioned that Celedant was in the dwarvan occupied mountains.

Sellis thought perhaps he had been a part of the battle and had been killed. If that were the happy case, Sellis figured that Melgor would never know who killed the wizard. That would leave him to collect the reward without doing a thing, and that would be most preferable as far as he was concerned.

If Melgor was on the run, though, Sellis assumed this Celedant must be powerful. He wasn't too keen about coming up against such a formidable wizard.

Sellis wanted to increase his own treasury, but he also felt obligated to Melgor. He owed the warlock a great debt because Melgor had gotten him off Dragon Isle before his misdeeds were uncovered. Sellis had stumbled upon the Academy's treasure vault and had decided to filch small amounts of gold over a long period of time by using his ring of teleportation, Nashmeol, a family heirloom.

Although no one had raised an alarm about the missing treasure, he knew it was only a matter of time before he was discovered and punished for his misdeeds. So, for a small price, Melgor had secretly ferried the warlock thief off the Isle and sent him on a trader ship. All he asked in return was a favor at some later date. He now had called that favor in. Kill Celedant.

This made Sellis wary. He never dreamed that the favor might lead to someone's death, especially a wizard's. And he did not like his own proximity to the deed. The obvious answer was to get someone else to do the killing and so leave Sellis free and clear.

But who would that person be, Sellis wondered? That was the key question.

He contemplated those he might use and finally came up with a warlock and a sorceress who lived a day's ride outside Partha. Those two were always on the lookout for gold and Sellis thought for sure that he could persuade them to attempt the attack on Celedant.

Using his ring, his one prized possession, he pictured a path that led to their farm and he teleported to their home. The ring allowed him the opportunity to move about quickly and quietly, but it also was good for finding treasure. All he needed was to see the place he wanted to travel to and he could teleport there later.

In the matter of the wizard's vaults, he had taken a great risk doing that. He had imagined a clear floor behind the door and had teleported inside. Sellis had been lucky. He appeared in the center of the room.

He could have ended up sticking halfway out of a wall…or something worse.

Sellis now walked up to a dilapidated house and called out.

"Griswald! Melody! You have a visitor."

"What do you want?" came a crusty reply.

"It is Sellis," the warlock answered.

A man, Griswald by name, looked out the door. He had wild curly hair that had not seen a brush for what look like years and his face was wrinkled with age.

"What would Sellis be doing here?" he asked. "You're not him. Now go away."

Sellis heard a commotion inside the house, followed by someone shoving the man out of the way. An equally old woman appeared. She stared at Sellis for several clicks of the clock.

"Well, if it isn't you, Sellis. Come on inside," she said with a cackle.

Sellis was well aware of the conditions of the house and he dreaded stepping foot inside the abode. He could already smell the rot and decay that permeated everything. He walked assuredly up to the front door, and the sorceress beckoned him in. The house consisted of a single room with all manner of things piled about in it.

Stepping inside Sellis could feel fleas crawling up his legs after only a few clicks of the clock. A table of beakers and vials containing various liquids gave off a noxious odor. Hanging from the cross beams were an assortment of herbs, all in bundles. It took Sellis all his fortitude to remain in the house longer than a few moments.

"Good day to you. I hope you are fine," he said politely.

The man grunted and Melody the sorceress smiled a toothless expression. "Aye, our business is in order."

"Good. Good," Sellis said.

"Why are you here, Sellis?" Griswald asked.

"If you're interested, I have a job for you," he said.

Both their heads bobbed up and down.

"What's it to be and how much will we get?" Melody asked, lisping excitedly. A bit of spittle appeared at the corner of her mouth.

Sellis smiled. "Always to the point, my dear. It's fifty to start and fifty at the end."

"Who do you want us to kill?" asked Griswald.

"I need you to eliminate a competitor. A wizard newly released from Dragon Isle."

Sellis knew that both Griswald and Melody had not been accepted on the Isle as youths and they hated everything to do with the wizards from that place.

"Humm, that sounds like fun," Melody said, licking her lips.

Griswald, however, did not agree. "A wizard out of the Isle? I think a hundred up front and a hundred at the end is more like the right price."

"Now, now," Sellis cautioned. "Let's not get carried away. This is a fledging wizard. Easy money for the likes of you two."

"A hundred," Melody stated. "Yes, I like that number much better."

Sellis sighed. It was the same game they always played, "I'll give you seventy-five, but that's the highest I can go. No more. Otherwise, I'll get someone else to kill the young one."

They both nodded. "We'll take the job for eighty which is a fair price, mind you. Thank you for the gold." Griswald held his hand out.

Sellis smiled and handed out four small pouches containing the gold.

"There," he said. "The wizard will be in town within a week. Once he arrives, I'll send word."

They both smiled and Sellis wondered if he'd rather be toothless like Melody or have rotten teeth like Griswald.

He exited the grungy house. The fleas were now above his knees, and he tried without much luck to brush them off.

"Well," he thought, "there goes another set of clothes. I paid the filth more than they are worth, but if they get the job done, it will save me a lot of problems."

He cast a cleansing spell that caused the fleas to die and drop off. His leggings were fresh now and devoid of the grime that saturated the house. More importantly, the spell removed the stench that had permeated the fabric. Eyeing his handiwork, he figured that his clothing might be saved after all.

Sellis thought about a hidden place near the main gate to Partha and he teleported there. He spread money about to the gate guards so they'd inform him of Celedant's arrival. He knew full well that Melgor would eventually reimburse him or at the very least, now owe him a huge favor.

Sellis then entered Partha, walked to his comfortable house near the main gate, and settled in to wait.

Later Sellis sat looking over the latest acquisition to his library. He had used his ring to teleport into a rival's home and purloin the tome.

A loud knock at his door brought him to his feet. He set the book on the side table, made his way to the door, and opened it to face a panting guard.

"The one called Celedant has arrived," the one-eyed man informed him. "Or at least the description fits. He is traveling with a dwarf and what we think are two wood elves."

Sellis thanked him with a small pouch of silver and shut the door. Focusing on the ring Nashmeol, he envisioned the yard outside the dilapidated house of Griswald and Melody. A single click of the clock later, he stood at their front door and rapped sharply.

The door cracked open.

Melody showed her toothless smile. "What is it this time, Sellis?"

"Celedant has arrived," he told her. "You can inquire about his whereabouts at the main gate."

Before she could answer, he was gone, whisked in the blink of an eye back to his comfortable home. He quickly packed a satchel filled with his most precious belongings. If his cohorts were caught, they would waste no time telling the authorities who had hired them and where he lived. Once he finished gathering his most important items, he focused on the ring, and blinked out of sight.

This Zeiglon affair had him on edge. A vacation was in order, and he wanted to be as far away from Partha as possible.

The disreputable Griswald drove his rickety wagon, drawn by a swayback donkey, up to the gate. The guards had to cover their noses as he approached.

"What do you need, old man?" the sergeant coughed.

"This and that," Griswald replied. "I have a friend, Celedant by name. You wouldn't know where he be staying, would you?"

Nearly choking over the smell, the sergeant answered quickly.

"I'm told he's staying at the Golden Flask Tavern. Now get this rotten wagon away from my gate." The guards were happy to have the odiferous wagon and its driver gone and they returned to their duty of seeing to the gate and its traffic.

The wagon slowly parted the crowded street on its way to the market, but there was one stop to make before setting up their wares. Griswald and Melody, who was hidden in the back of the wagon, wound their way through the traffic toward the inn. Tact was not in the two magic users' vocabulary, and they parked their wagon at the front door and tied their bone-weary mule up to the inn's hitching post.

They both got down from the wagon and their smell preceded them as they entered the inn. The owner behind the bar gagged as they entered.

"You two! Out with you," the bar owner shouted. "Don't come back until you bathe and get clean clothes."

The husband and wife cackled at that. "Tell the wizard, Celedant, we await him in the market," Griswald said.

The two exited the building, much to the proprietor's relief. They turned their wagon around and headed to the market, where they were given wide birth and a clear area to set up shop. No one dared attempt sell anything near them. Even the beggars gave them a wide berth and switched to the other side of the square to seek alms.

Griswald and Melody set up a table with dented pots and pans for sale as well as an assortment of medicinal herbs. They put out a placard that read, in Melody's horrific writing, "All your magical healing needs."

CHAPTER SIXTEEN

I t had been two years since the capture of Prince Aedith. All the correspondence sent by the elves had been rebuked by King Zachary. Then, finally, he relented and sent word that the elves could send one envoy to plead for the prince's life.

Treakis was chosen, an elf well-versed in the actions of men and knowledgeable of the political tensions in the south. He was burley for an elf, but as eloquent as their most renowned ambassadors.

Treakis undertook his duty leading a troop of elven horse guards, and they quickly covered the vast distance from the wood elves' forested stronghold to the kingdom of Zeiglon. He was allowed to enter the city immediately and was given a vacant townhouse to stay in. His company of soldiers elected to stay outside of the city.

The Zeiglon advisors assured him that it would be but a few days before he was called to speak with the emperor. Treakis waited and waited and several weeks had passed before a captain of the royal guard came to get him for an audience with the king.

As the elf entered the palace proper, he saw that everything had been adorned in black. The whole city had the feel of a perpetual gloomy night. He was led to the throne room, where Zachary sat on the despised shell throne of Zeiglon. Treakis was not sure what to make of the three rods highchair or the shells fanning out behind the king like peacock feathers.

Zachary motioned to the elf. "What might Zeiglon do for you, master elf."

Treakis centered himself and spoke with the proper decorum.

"I have been sent to negotiate the release of Prince Aedith, currently being attended to by your highness."

The king sat there several moments before he spoke.

"Alright. I will consider this. Now please return to your house for I have pressing business to attend to."

Treakis nodded politely and backed out of the chamber.

The cat and mouse gamesmanship between them went on for months. The king was forever dragging it out, longer and longer, but being an elf, Treakis was willing to wait. The passage of time did not bother him. He and the Prince could wait out the king.

Treakis, however, became concerned about how his prince might presently be being kept, and he knew he could not play the waiting game forever.

Celedant and his companions did not receive the message from the barman about Griswald and Melody until they had come back late that night. The proprietor warned them of the disreputable looks of the two and then fed them a wonderful meal.

Celedant had to admit that Goran had a habit of knowing the very best places to stay and eat. Gwendolyn agreed and patted the dwarf's belly to emphasize her statement. The four decided that they would wait until morning before going to the market, and they settled in for a good night's sleep.

It was a rainy miserable night and Celedant slept with his windows closed. In the middle of the night he awoke to the hushed sounds of talking and he heard a rattle at his window. He arose, made his way to the window, and called forth a light spell to illuminate the crystal on his staff's head.

There in the window he saw a face that quickly ducked away, followed by a screech and a clatter.

He threw open the window and looked down into the darkened alley that ran along the side of the Inn. He saw two figures lying tangled in a broken ladder, and then a bright light coalesced in front of one of the prone figures before it shot upward.

A ball of energy rushed toward Celedant and the wizard threw himself inside the room as the spell missed him and went on upward to blow a sizable chunk in the overhanging roof. Then smaller balls of energy came up and splattered around the window and finally passed through it. Small patches of fire lit up the room and Celedant blew them out with a wind spell.

By this time Azimuth, Gwendolyn and Goran had entered his room with quizzical looks on their faces. Celedant looked bemused.

"Two inept warlocks are trying their best to annoy my sleep," he said.

Goran ran out of the room followed by the other two. Celedant snuck over to the window, extended his hand and dropped small balls of fire down on the attacking warlocks. He heard several yelps of pain, and then the full-scale scuffle that was breaking out.

Celedant chanced a peek out the window. Below him Goran and Azimuth had the warlocks at bay against the wall, holding them securely, their weapons at their throats. Gwendolyn held her bow string tightly with an arrow aimed at the two miscreants.

Celedant rushed down to the alley as the innkeeper ran out the front door with a lamp, accompanied by some of the besotted, late-night patrons, curious as to what all the commotion was about. The wizard was close on his heels.

Turning the corner, Celedant saw in the owner's lamp light that Azimuth and Goran had trapped two of what were the filthiest warlocks he had ever seen. The odor of them hid whatever smell the alley itself was putting out. The source of the putrid smell, a filthy warlock and a sorcerous, were cackling toothlessly at them all. It was only by the lamp light that Celedant could tell that one of the laughing warlocks was actually a woman.

"Look here, Celedant. Two rats sent to kill you," Goran announced.

The words had barely left his lips when he and Azimuth were shoved backward and slammed against the other wall of the narrow alley and held in place against it by a vine-like substance that only tangled them up further when they tried to escape.

Celedant wasted no time and sent a holding spell at the warlocks, but the woman made a waving gesture and the spell passed harmlessly by them. She then cast a summoning spell that brought forth two orcs that appeared before Celedant and attacked him.

The wizard fended off the two with his staff while he drew his sword. Gwendolyn shot an arrow, aimed at Melody, but the evil sorceress saw the arrow and erected a shield wall in front of her. When the arrow struck the magical shield, it was deflected downward, just missing her foot by inches.

The two warlocks now moved to the middle of the alley and cast several spells.

Celedant had finished off the two orcs in short order, but the warlocks continued casting other spells. Celedant dove to his right behind a pile of garbage as their spells passed over him. Cautiously, he looked out past the noxious waste and saw the warlocks' spells impact one of the helpless patrons and turn him to stone.

Celedant called forth his power and sent a wave of magical energy toward the two. Griswald and Melody were thrown backward, head over heels, and tumbled along the cobbled street.

Goran had not stopped struggling against the wall he and Azimuth were still pinned to. He managed to retrieve a small vial from his pouch and got it up to his mouth. He pulled out the cork with his teeth and poured the substance over the entangling vines. The vines dissolved, and he was free. He took two quick steps over toward the fallen Griswald.

With everyone's attention elsewhere, Azimuth had used some of his draconic power to set himself free. Opening his mouth, he spewed fire at the vines, burning them to a crisp and leaving him unscathed. He took a moment to grin ferociously. He had not known he could use his fire in his elven state, but he had for long been thinking about it and wanting to try. It worked, but he would have to be cautious not to let anyone but Celedant see him do it.

Goran placed the edge of his axe against the Griswald's neck. "Slow down, my friend, or yer head will be separated from yer body."

Melody yelped in terror and crawled away from her foul smelling mate until her back was against the alley wall.

Celedant stepped over the broken ladder, his senses still assaulted by the couple's odor.

"Who sent you?" he asked them.

They both laughed insanely.

"You don't know who," the man jeered. "Ha, ha. You don't know who."

"Ye'll tell us...or I'll split yer belly," Goran said menacingly.

Griswald shook his head. "I don't fear you, master dwarf."

"They smell to high heaven," Azimuth said. "We should dunk them in water to get some of the grime off...and to see who we're talking to."

His words elicited a pleading cry from the sorceress.

The warlock wailed a simple, "Noooo!"

"I have a horse trough that will fit both of them," the innkeeper said. "We can scrub them down to where at least we can talk to them without gagging."

Melody kept wailing, "No, no, no!"

"Come," Goran said and grabbed Griswald by the nape of the neck.

"I'll talk. Just no bath, please," the warlock pleaded.

Celedant stepped forward, ignoring the rancid odor.

"Tell me who sent you or nothing will keep you from having a bath."

"Sellis did. Sellis did," the woman said.

"Who is this Sellis?" Azimuth asked, having never heard of the man.

The warlock looked askance at his wife, but continued for her. "Sellis comes around whenever he had odd jobs for us to do."

"Killing is an odd job?" Goran asked.

Griswald answered with a shrug. "Killing is the oddest of all, but if the price is right...."

"So, you do a lot of killing for this Sellis?" Celedant asked.

"Yes," the sorceress replied, but Griswald shouted, "No!"

A captain of the city's night guards, alerted by the magical commotion, turned up at the mouth of the alley.

"What goes on here?" the captain asked.

"These two vagabonds attacked us and they damaged the inn. They also turned this poor fellow to stone," Azimuth answered and pointed to the frozen patron.

"Hmm," the guardsman said, eyeing the unlucky patron. "I'll get to the bottom of this."

Celedant walked over and retrieved a book of spells from the warlock's satchel.

"Never mind. I can handle this." He flipped through the pages and came to the right spell.

Soon the patron was sitting up on the sidewalk, his hands on his head. The wizard assured him that the headache from the spell would go away by morning, but the headache he had from all the brew he had imbibed would not.

The patron began slurring his story to the guard when a dark black smoke rose up and enveloped them all. Celedant heard a clatter of weapons and a yell, "They're getting away!"

Gwendolyn sent two arrows speeding into the dark, but she only heard them bounce off a nearby stone building,

The smoke was so black in the night's gloomy drizzle that no one could see anyone else. Celedant called forth the same spell he had used to put out the flames in his room and added a little bit of extra power to it and the dark smoke was blown away.

Both the foul, magic-using warlocks had escaped. The two guards who had been holding them were unconscious on the ally's grubby cobblestones.

More guards arrived and began a search, but Celedant doubted they would find the warlock and sorceress.

He and his friends retired to the inn. The innkeeper poured them each a glass of red wine and they sat at the bar to drink. Around them the late-night patrons stumbled back to their tables.

"Yer sure are popular, Celedant," Goran said. "Good thing those two were lousy killers and easily dealt with. Otherwise they might have caught ye fast asleep."

"Like we've said before, these attacks seem to be of several different types," Azimuth added. "I myself believe that you have two or three people all trying to kill you at once."

"Well, let's hope this will be the last of it." Celedant said. "I grow weary of keeping my eyes peeled for threats around every corner."

After they had battled these deranged pair of wizards, the wine allowed them to relax. They retired to their beds, and soon were asleep, except Azimuth. He spent the remainder of the night patrolling outside the inn.

CHAPTER SEVENTEEN

T he following day the four of them made their way to the King of Partha's enormous castle. When they arrived, Celedant asked to see the Lord Chancellor. The guards looked askance at them, but nevertheless took his request into the castle.

"The message from Capres did not cover anything for me to convey to the King," Celedant said to the others. "Do I just fabricate a reason as to why we are here?"

Azimuth shook his head. "No. Tell them you have been sent to assess the situation between Partha and Zeiglon and to report back to Dragon Isle. That should be enough to keep the king talking for many turns of the clock."

A full turn of the clock did pass before word reached them that the Chancellor would meet with them.

He ushered them into his office and shut the door behind them. He was a whipcord thin man with a long mustache that drooped down over his jaws.

"Welcome, Celedant…and the rest of you," the Chancellor said in a most gracious manner.

"I owe you much for seeing us so soon," Celedant replied.

"No," came the reply. "There is much debate about Zeiglon and their intentions towards Partha. A wizard from the fabled Dragon Isle is most welcome. Our last Court Wizard fell sick and died recently...under suspicious circumstances. A letter has been dispatched north to see if the Isle can be of help. But you have now shown up on our doorstep."

"Our deepest condolences for the demise of your court wizard," the Celedant said, "but I have not been sent to replace him. I am newly on the road and cannot be of any useful service to a king. An older and much wiser wizard would be better."

"Ah, with war looming," the Chancellor said, "you are what we have, and so you must do."

Azimuth leaned forward. "What of Zeiglon?"

The chancellor sighed. "That is the true question. I wish I knew." He stood up. "Duty calls. Come to the castle tomorrow morning, and I'll get you in to see the king."

The four exited the castle.

"I don't like what he suggested about Zeiglon and their intentions," Azimuth said.

"It's more what he did not tell us that has me troubled," Goran added.

"I don't like the fact that the last wizard was—we can assume— killed. We need to be extra careful if Zeiglon's agents are still nosing about," Celedant warned.

The others agreed. They planned not to let any one of them wander off by themselves, no matter what the cause.

The next day the four travelers walked up to the keep. Celedant wore his cleanest clothes, a long cloak that came down to his ankles, and he wore his brown hair loose about his shoulders. His staff clicked decisively along on the cobbled street. Azimuth was dressed immaculately in red. Goran wore his mail and carried his axe on his shoulder. Gwendolyn wore a deep forest green cloak that covered leather armor.

The guards at the gate called for a messenger to alert those inside before he let them pass.

Once inside the keep, they couldn't help but admire its fine stonework. Even Goran noted that it was almost as good as dwarven work.

A soldier wearing plate mail armor met them at the first stone steps of the keep and motioned them to follow him through giant double doors. They were led past the main hall to a smaller room where a table and chairs had been placed.

They stood behind their chairs until a tall, stern looking man entered.

"King Haruldi," the soldier called out.

An older man, dressed in the official robes of office, walked in and promptly eyed the group. He spotted Celedant and greeted him.

"I welcome you, wizard of the fabled Dragon Isle. Come sit at my table. There is no need for formal speech here."

"I am pleased to be at your service, my lord," Celedant said. "The Master Wizards of Dragon Isle send their best wishes."

The king grimaced. "I but wish the Isles were closer to my shores. I could use their help right now."

"I, too, am from the Isles," Azimuth announced, "but, alas, not a wizard. Why do you wish so?"

"I seek counsel regarding the country of Zeiglon," replied the King.

"Zeiglon has many of my masters worried, as well," Celedant quickly added.

"Yes," King Haruldi said. "They are forever threatening to invade and could easily overrun my country, should they decide to do so."

"Are they going to invade?" Goran asked.

"It's not a question of are, but when. They have already taken our western most outpost and turned it into a fortress." the king said sadly. "Curse them. They send their troops to trespass on our lands dressed as mercenaries who attack our outposts and harass the populace."

"It is not in the Isle's best interest for Zeiglon to start a war," Celedant declared. "I will put myself at your disposal, should any problems arise."

"Certainly, it would be a great burden off my shoulders to have a wizard of the Isle to advise me in these troubled times," the king said, bowing his head to acknowledge his respect for the wizard.

Celedant bowed back. "I understand, my lord."

Halsbred had watched with disgust when he saw Celedant ride into Partha.

He had been sure the ogres would have been successful, but such was his recent luck that he and his three remaining mercenaries had to take rooms in an inn near the main gate of Partha. There they could take turns watching the road from the north.

Halsbred was relieved that at least the mercenaries were good at watching. They had proven of little use otherwise, except for spending his gold.

He had waited days for reports about Celedant and his companions, and then a recent rumor began to spread through the populace that the king had appointed a new wizard to his council. It took just a few questions to find out that was Celedant, who, Halsbred learned, had befriended the King. He wondered now if that might have been Dragon Isle's reason for sending Celedant south.

The problematic thing for him was that his target was now ensconced within Partha's Castle, and that provided Halsbred little opportunity to act by himself.

He could think of no other way to handle this new situation than to hire someone to penetrate the castle's defenses and attack the wizard. But who?

He snapped his fingers. The city had to have an assassin's guild. Most of the large cities had one and they were all connected in one way or another. Contacting the secret group could prove to be a problem, though. It was not the sort of job that one hung out a placard advertising for business. Halsbred would have to be the one to make contact with them and there was only one way to do it. He had to start from the ground up and work his way into that guild.

Halsbred knew there was a guild system at work in all the cities—from the sewer sweepers, to the beggars, even to the thieves. He had to use one of these more assessable guilds to find the assassins.

He went to the central plaza of the city to watch the people closely and he finally spotted a beggar who stood out among the others. There was something different about him that Halsbred just could not put his finger on, but he decided to examine the man closer. He then realized this beggar looked better off than the other beggars near him. His ragged appearance seemed more of a show. His coat was old and tattered, but well-made, and his beard was also scruffy, but if it were brushed out, it would be very passable. Halsbred thought he looked more like a manager of others than a beggar of them.

Halsbred approached the man, dropped a gold coin into the man's bowl, and whispered to him.

"I have business for the assassins."

Having said that simple phrase, he turned and walked away. The beggar quickly scooped up the coin and deposited in his scruffy coat. Then he stood up and disappeared into the crowd. The beggar wove his way in and out of the crowd to throw off anyone following him before he ducked onto a smaller side street and disappeared through a doorway.

Halsbred made sure that, during the following days, he was seen hanging around the city center before he strolled back to the inn in plain sight. It would be only a matter of time before he was contacted. By whom was another matter. It would simply be a matter of who wanted the most gold for leading him to the right people.

One evening, as the warlock sat eating his dinner in the common room of a fine inn, a foppish man, dressed in the latest fashion, entered the room and stood before Halsbred. The warlock looked up and motioned the man to take a seat.

The man sat. "I hear that you are looking for someone."

Halsbred smiled. His gambit had worked.

"I have work to offer…for the right person," he said in a discrete local dialect.

"Well," the foppish man said, "I may be able to help you. If you will, come with me."

The man stood and shoved his way through the crowd towards the door. Halsbred threw a coin on the table and followed.

Out in the street the warlock caught up with the man and fell into step beside him. They left the section of town where Halsbred's inn was situated and wound their way down the street to the docks. The waterfront was located along a narrow beach. The castle had been built well above it to protect the shoreline from invasions.

The further they went, the darker the streets became, and the warlock became tense and was getting worried. He already had a dozen spells running through his mind to meet whatever situation occurred, something that had been drummed into his head again and again as a student of Dragon Isle. It was one of the best things he had learned during his early schooling.

Approaching a rundown shop, he followed his guide inside. A huge man sat behind a counter. The smell of spices was so strong in the little room it nearly made Halsbred cough. There were small glass jars all around the shop containing a multitude of spices from around the world.

The proprietor barely acknowledged the two and they walked straight through the store to a back door.

The man Halsbred was following stopped for a single click of a clock and issued a warning to the warlock.

"Try any spell, and you'll be dead before you can cast it. Try anything else, and you're dead just the same. Follow me."

Halsbred figured that he was in one of the assassins' meeting places. They probably had a dozen such sites around the city, places where they could bring people and not risk giving away their base.

The warlock nodded, and the man opened the door to a small back alley. They exited the building and ducked into the doorway of what looked like an abandoned building. The smell of mold accosted Halsbred's senses as the other man led him through to a door on the other side of the building. He opened the door for Halsbred.

"Go through this door and enter the next. Then wait."

Halsbred stepped over to the door and opened it. Inside was a small room with a table and four chairs. He took a seat, his back to the wall, and watched the doorway, listening for any sound.

Without warning, the door opened and a rotund woman wearing a fashionable dress stepped inside the room. She sat down across from him and gave him a slight nod as if acknowledging that he had chosen the safest chair. Halsbred smiled. This was exactly what an assassin would do.

"What do you want?" she asked him.

The warlock looked her over.

"Were you expecting something else?" she asked amused.

"Well, yes, I was," Halsbred replied honestly.

She smiled, her teeth sparkling in the lamplight. "I must move in all circles of society, but I am who you see – the picture of a respectful woman. Come now. Time for business."

The warlock got right to his point. "I need a man killed."

"That is what we do best. Who and why?" she said in the sweetest of tones.

"The new wizard at the castle, Celedant," Halsbred replied. "As for the why, I have my own personal reasons."

"I have no need to know why you want this man killed. I'm also concerned with the golden side of this business." She laughed. "Getting into the castle will cost you, my friend."

He looked at her, hard, "I am more than willing to pay."

"I could kill you now and have your money, but that would give us a bad name for future business," the smartly dressed woman informed him. Her voice was now cold. "The price is non-negotiable. Five hundred in gold or the equivalent. We will pick when to strike, and there will be no more contact after tonight."

Halsbred pulled forth a small pouch. "Will diamonds be a sufficient form of payment?"

She smiled wickedly.

"I take all types of payments, darling." Her tone was sweet again. She emptied the pouch on the table and sorted through the diamonds before putting them back into their container. "These are of fine quality."

She pocketed the pouch.

"When will I know it is done?" Halsbred asked.

"Just keep an ear out on the street," she replied. "Something this ambitious will make big news. Now, my man is waiting for you outside. He will take you back to the inn. Our business here is concluded."

Celedant and his friends had immediately moved into the castle. Each had their own austere room consisting of a bunk, a chest, and a small writing table.

To a wizard, used to such conditions of his cell on Dragon Isle, it was of no concern. Azimuth had no problem with his room, either, but his heightened sense of smell left him liking the room a bit less. It smelled of mice and rotten wood, and he would have preferred to revert to his dragon form and curl around the spires on the roof to enjoy the fresh night air. Goran, used to the harsh conditions of the world, found any bed out of the rain of great comfort, but Gwendolyn felt like she was trapped in a cage. Like Azimuth, she was used to the outdoors, although being inside here, not too far from Celedant, she thought, was no burden to her.

Celedant's job turned out to be boring beyond belief. The king would sit on his high throne in his official red robes of state and judge the most serious crimes committed in the city. Celedant was rarely of consequence to him, but as the king's advisor and court wizard, he had to be present.

Meanwhile Azimuth, Gwendolyn and Goran had free access to the castle and wandered around it and around the city. At night, Azimuth would take to the skies, his magnificent dragon form reveling in the freedom, his heart soaring. While he knew it was important for him to accompany his friend and partner on this mission, maintaining his elven form had felt constricting and confining.

One night he was interrupted as soon as he had changed form.

Ah, just as I suspected. A voice came to him telepathically. Never having heard it before, he turned his head to see who had discovered him.

Gwendolyn?

One and the same.

How did you know? he asked her.

You forget that I, too, have been around dragons before. Aside from the wizards of Dragon Isle, the elves are the only ones who know the secret of the dragons and of their ability to change forms, and that in fact they are much grander than the firedrakes other folks think they are.

Pfft! Fire drakes. Tiny imitations of dragonkind with little intelligence or sense.

Gwendolyn laughed. *How right you are, my friend. Do you do this every night?*

As much as I can, although it is not always possible, in part because I don't always have enough space to return to my dragon form.

That's unfortunate. It must be very confining to go from such a massive size down to elven or wolf size.

It is, he agreed. *I don't wish to be rude, but I am anxious to take flight. At the same time, I would love to continue our conversation. While I do also know sign language, it is still so much easier to speak mind-to-mind with you. Would you like to go with me?*

His question shocked her. Never in all her years had she ever entertained the idea of riding a dragon. Her bravery made her want to try, but without a saddle, it would be sheer suicide.

Sensing her hesitation, Azimuth spoke a word of magic, and a saddle appeared on him.

Once again, Gwendolyn was amazed. *Did you read my mind, even though I did not voice my concern?*

Azimuth gave her a big, draconic grin. *If you like, I can elevate you up into the saddle.*

Her eyes as big as saucers, she smiled. *Yes, please!*

For the next several hours the two of them soared over the countryside. She didn't even mind when he stopped to eat a couple of deer he slew.

They had a long and deep conversation, thrilling to Gwendolyn. Never in her life had she been able to converse so freely or for so long with another. It was a night she would never forget.

One afternoon, when Gwendolyn, Azimuth and Goran were alone in one of the castle's towers, Goran had been considering their situation and made a thoughtful comment to Azimuth.

"I would not want to defend this city in a siege," he said. "There are barely enough men to guard the outer wall."

Azimuth agreed. "Before a siege took place, I would evacuate to the north and leave the city open to the invaders."

Unbeknownst to Goran, the dragon was speaking from first-hand knowledge, having scouted out the city thoroughly from above.

Gwendolyn signed to Goran. "If they stay and fight, there will be much loss of life."

"We should tell Celedant of this," the dwarf said. "Maybe the king will then see the wisdom,"

"It is hard to leave a city that one has governed for so many years," Azimuth said. "I doubt that even a master wizard would be able to persuade the king. Still, Celedant must try."

Night descended on the city, enveloping it in complete darkness.

Celedant was late as he quickly walked down the corridors on his way to the king's private meeting room. It was lucky he was running late for when he turned the corner, he saw four men gathered around the door to the meeting room, their weapons drawn.

He stopped in his tracks. "Hoy! What's this about?"

The man closest to him turned and Celedant could see that the man was thinking about what to do next. But not for long, Celedant thought, and he charged, his sword raised high. The wizard then slid to the side and parried the man's sword with a stroke of his staff. As the man fell forward, Celedant clouted the assassin firmly on the head with his staff.

The other three burst into action. One came at the wizard while the other two forced the door of the meeting room open with their shoulders. There were cries from within the room, but Celedant could do little for those inside. He had to deal with the charging man bent on killing him.

He quickly cast a simple spell, and the man slid and fell on the greasy substance that suddenly appeared on the floor. The assassin swung his blade to keep the wizard at bay, but Celedant did not have to get any closer to the man. Instead he cast another spell, this time a bit more complicated one, and a small sphere a light arched from his staff to impact and fell the man. Celedant did not know if the man was dead or not, but he was lying prone and he was not moving.

Celedant now moved quickly past the assassin and into the meeting room. Two attackers had the king hemmed into the corner of the room where he was desperately defending himself. Celedant could see the chamberlain lying in a pool of blood and another of King Haruldi's advisors leaning against the wall trying with his sleeve to staunch the flow of blood from a serious wound.

The wizard from Dragon Isle stepped past the wounded man and stepped around the table. He used his staff like a spear, not really knowing what else to do, and the butt of his staff struck one attacker in the kidneys. He doubled over in pain. Celedant then used the other end of the staff to knock him unconscious. With that assailant down, the king turned his attention to the final attacker and went on the offensive.

Their swords flashed and clanged and the men stood toe-to-toe and fought.

After spotting an opening in the invader's defense, the king then slipped his sword under the man's guard and neatly penetrated the leather armor, entering the man's heart. The attacker fell immediately, clutching the bloody hole.

The king turned, expecting more attackers, but there were no more.

"I took care of two in the hallway," Celedant assured him. "I believe this was the last of the assassins."

King Haruldi was gasping for breath.

"I've not had a workout like that in years, he said. "That bastard of a chamberlain was in on the attacks. Tried to slit my throat, he did, but I handled him. That was before the door crashed open and I was attacked by these vermin."

Neither the king nor the wizard knew that the assassins had believed that Celedant had been in the chamber. His lateness had saved both his and the King's life.

When the guards finally arrived in the room, Haruldi ordered them, "There is one alive here. Get aid for the general."

"There are also two in the hallway that I knocked out," Celedant added.

The guard returned with bad news.

"There is only one man in the hallway, and he is dead."

"Damn," echoed both the king and Celedant. "He will get word back to their leaders that their attack failed," Celedant said.

"Search the grounds and see if you can find him," the king ordered.

"Yes, my lord," the guard answered.

CHAPTER EIGHTEEN

King Haruldi motioned to Celedant.

"Come. Follow me to a safer place where we can talk in private."

Five guards fell in behind the king and escorted them both to safety.

They soon found themselves in a windowless room that was well below ground, its steps slick with dampness, its air slightly stale.

"Celedant, I am sorry for such quarters," the King apologized, "but with what happened in the meeting room, I deem it safer to meet here in secret. The guards will keep us safe. And by the way, you're no mean fighter yourself."

The wizard took a chair.

"No need to apologize, my lord. After what just transpired, I believe this is necessary too. Your own household has been compromised. You should know that I have been troubled by attempts on my life ever since I left Trondheim."

"It's as I feared," the King stated. "It seems that war will follow. There can be no other reason to kill me, or you, other than to leave the country in shambles."

Celedant steeled himself as he broached his touchy subject.

"My friends have reported to me that you are incapable of manning the walls sufficiently should an enemy besiege the city."

Haruldi nodded sadly. "It is true. Most of my soldiers are stationed at outposts along the border with Zeiglon. They could never be recalled in time."

"Do you have a plan in place?" Celedant asked.

"That was the purpose of this meeting," the King said. "I wanted your input in deciding what the best course of action would be, should the enemy cross the lower border. They already control the north."

"Can a city of this size be evacuated?" Celedant asked. "I'm afraid I have no experience in such matters."

"It depends on how much time we have. Many will stay, but most can exit the city. The ships are capable of carrying most of our people to safety. But where does the entire population of a city go?"

"They can go north," the wizard answered slowly after some consideration. "The forest and foothills would be a good place to hide."

Haruldi shook his head. "That would be fine for country folk, but these people are city raised. They cannot survive in the wild. And what food we could take would not last long."

The wizard snapped his fingers as a thought lit up his eyes.

"You could go to the dwarves! I recently did Gilbert and the Stonesplitter Clan a great favor. They would at least be able to shelter you for a time."

"Oh, I won't be going," Haruldi said. "My son and I will ride to battle with my horsemen. My daughter will oversee the evacuation. Kinemark, my son, is presently out on patrol, but I'll send a message to him to return immediately. Both my children are more than reliable in a crisis. The guard will follow them, and the people will, as well."

He went to the door and opened it and commanded one of the guards to bring in his daughter. They waited several clicks of the clock before there was a knock on the door, and Eleanor, the king's daughter, entered.

Celedant admired the glorious waves of long auburn hair that fell to the middle of her back. Her eyes were a beautiful shade of green.

"Sorry for keeping you waiting," she apologized, "but I was in the horse stables when the attackers came after you. I wasn't able to find you in the castle anywhere."

"That is all right, my daughter," her father assured her. "I want to present to you Celedant, the wizard I have told you about."

She curtsied. "I have seen you about the castle. It is a pleasure to meet you."

Celedant bowed and replied, "The pleasure is mine."

The king interrupted. "Eleanor. Celedant and I have been discussing the Zeiglon problem. If they are bold enough to send assassins—and we will know that soon enough from the one Celedant knocked out—it means they are bold enough to attack sooner rather than later. We must be prepared. The city cannot be defended against the host that Zeiglon will send. We must ready the people to evacuate the city and go north into the mountains. Celedant has had dealings with the dwarvan Stonesplitter clan and he's certain that Gilbert will help us in our time of need."

"Why are telling me this?" she asked.

"Because your brother and I will be riding to battle, and you will lead the people to safety," Haruldi informed her.

"But..." she began.

The king cut her off.

"I know what you would ask of me, but you may not ride with us. Yours will be the more important mission, keeping our people safe."

Celedant interrupted. "Princess Eleanor, your father is right, you know. The people must be protected, and that will fall onto your shoulders. There is no one else."

She acquiesced. "I understand. Do you know when the attack will come?"

"No," King Haruldi replied. "We have no idea, but so brash an attack in my own household as just occurred tells me that it will come soon enough. We must be prepared. I don't want the people to be worried. If they panic, that would be detrimental to our plans. When the moment to evacuate comes, the guards will issue the warning and the orders. Then you can lead the people to safety."

She nodded her head.

The king continued, "Go prepare what is needed for your journey. Then try and get some sleep. We need to be prepared for their attack at any moment. Rest assured that I am in good health."

"It has been a pleasure, Princess," Celedant said, bowing.

She blushed a bit.

As she departed, she said, "Both of you be careful."

The king looked over at the wizard.

"She is a headstrong girl, I have to say, and she vexes me greatly."

"She knows her duty. That is what makes her headstrong," Celedant said. "She is, after all, your daughter."

"Headstrong…or stubborn?" the King asked. "Is that what you're calling me?"

The wizard laughed. "But, of course, my lord…both!"

"Come," the king said. "I have one last thing to show you."

He went over to the door where the guards still stood with their weapons drawn. Celedant followed. The king went through the doorway and descended deeper down more damp stairs into the bedrock that the castle had been built on. Eventually he stopped at a great iron-bound door.

He motioned to it. "I don't know why they make such strong doors. If a thief wants in, he'll find a way."

He retrieved a large key from his belt and inserted it into the lock. It turned easily on its well-oiled springs and he opened the door. In front of them was the treasure vault of the kingdom.

A guard discretely gave the king a torch and shut the door behind them. Haruldi took the torch and lit several others about the room. The vault contained many chests and the king went over to a particularly long one and opened it. Celedant could see that it contained a variety of weapons.

The king searched through the swords, daggers and other implements of war until he pulled forth a plain looking sword. He presented it to Celedant.

"This is Dragon Bolt, a sword of great age. It is—supposedly—magical. It hides its secrets well. It was entrusted to me to keep until the proper owner could be found. I think you should carry it into the battles to come. You can keep it safe, I know, for its future lies here with Partha." He handed the sword over to the young wizard. "You deserve a magical weapon. Being a wizard, you might also discover not only the one it was made for, but also, in time, discern its true power."

Celedant took the hilt and immediately felt the surge of magical energy that the sword possessed.

"I thank you, my lord," he said. "I can already feel the energy within this vessel. Sooner or later, I will fathom it out completely, but I am not sure I deserve such a weapon."

The king smiled. "For saving my life, you deserve more, but this is the best I can offer."

Celedant left the king in the hands of his guards and ascended back up to his own rooms

The next day after his meeting with the king, Celedant found his three friends on the outer parapet looking over the city.

As he approached them, Goran called out, "What have ye got there, wizard?"

Celedant looked at him. "A sword of course," he said blankly.

He tossed it to the dwarf. Goran caught it and hefted it appraisingly. He laughed.

"'Tis balanced," he said, "but dull and rusted. I think the king needed to get rid of it so instead of passing it off as scrap metal, he gave it to ye."

Azimuth laughed, too, took hold of the blade, but then nearly dropped it.

"My friend, this may look like the worst blade around," the dragon said, "but there is powerful magic stored within its steel."

Celedant smiled. "I had hoped someone would confirm that. I thought I might be a bit crazed when I touched it and felt its abilities."

"Let's go to the smithy and have him sharpen it a bit. Then we will see what it can do," Goran said.

They took two stairways down and entered the training portion of the castle. The smithy was located in the yard, against the outer wall. Dark smoke rose into the air from his furnace and had stained the whole wall above the shop. They walked over to the smith.

He looked dubiously at the blade, but began sharpening it. Beneath the rust a bright shiny edge began to appear.

"Let me see if I can clean the rust off the blade before you use it," the smithy said. "There may be a gem hiding underneath."

He gathered up a rough material and started scrubbing at the rust and it slowly began flaking off to reveal the bright blade previously hidden under it.

"See?" he said. "It's amazing what a thin layer of grime can hide. Tis a beautiful piece of work. Go out to the marshalling yard and see how it does against those training blocks."

The four friends walked over to several soldiers who were busy honing their skills as swordsmen on huge tree trunks that had been placed upright in the ground. Several of them nodded as the four approached.

Celedant stood in front of one of the trunks. The soldiers had stopped working out and were interested in what the wiry wizard could do. He placed the blade against the tree and gave it a soft blow. The blade bit into the wood and he quickly pulled it out, ready to give it a more powerful swing. At his second blow he could have sworn that the blade had blazed red for a second as it cut into the wood. There was a deep cut, and what should have been a difficult time for him to pull the blade out of the wood, wasn't. It slipped out easily.

Gwendolyn egged him on, signing, "Go ahead. Give it a real blow, not those love taps."

Goran laughed.

Azimuth laughed too. "Go ahead. Let the dwarf have his fun."

Celedant reared back and gave the sword a powerful swing. The blade glowed red hot and sliced completely through the thick trunk toppling the top half of the tree down to the courtyard.

A complete silence fell over the watchers

"Glad yer on me side," Goran said seriously,

Celedant backhanded the tree trunk this time and severed the top half. It flew into the air.

Azimuth laughed. "Enough showing off, my friend. Come let us have lunch and please belt that sword around your waist. A true swordsman does not carry it under his arm like a loaf of bread."

CHAPTER NINETEEN

I t was a dark morning when the horse and rider pounded through the gates to the castle. His urgent message immediately roused the king from his bed. Zeiglon had invaded and attacked one of the nearer outposts.

Haruldi sent messages to all the outlying garrisons. He planned to have all their horsemen meet at the great river crossing in three days' time, ready to ride against the invaders. In the city the troops readied their mounts as Haruldi assembled his knights.

Celedant, Azimuth, Gwendolyn and Goran, all who had now been thoroughly welcomed to the king's court, were asked to ride with Haruldi's command. It was a high honor seldom given to outsiders, but Haruldi had grown fond of the advice that Celedant gave him about the probable intentions of Zeiglon.

Before they rode out, Goran met separately with Gwendolyn. "I need ye to look after the princess. She is young and inexperienced in the ways of war and she will need your advice."

Gwendolyn's face turned red. She signed to the traveler with her fast hands and gave emphasis to each of her words. She wanted to go with the other three. She especially wanted to travel with and, if necessary, protect Celedant

The dwarf put his hand on her shoulder. "I know. I wouldna want to be left behind. But this war is bigger than the both of us. Ye will be the protector of the princess. Come. Celedant will introduce ye to Princess Eleanor."

As he passed Celedant's room, the wizard came out and fell into step with them.

"Going to see the princess," Goran said.

Celedant noticed the expression on Gwendolyn's face and knew better than to interrupt. When they arrived at Eleanor's suite of rooms, they met two guards standing at attention outside her door. Celedant walked right up to them.

"I am Celedant, Wizard from Dragon Isle, and these are my trusted friends. I am here to speak with the princess."

One guard disappeared into her room. The other loosened his sword, his hand ready to draw it. The other guard reappeared and then held the door open for the wizard.

The four found themselves in a room decorated by a unique feminine touch. Bright tapestries hung along the walls and flowers filled the room with a fragrant scent. The princess came into the room and allowed Celedant to kiss her hand before he formally introduced his companions.

"This reluctant dwarf is Goran," the wizard said, pulling Goran forward. "A famed traveler and warrior. The lady behind him is Gwendolyn, a half elf. She is a dead shot with her bow. This little fellow you can call Azimuth."

The princess bowed her head to the newcomers, and the wizard went on.

"I would like to offer Gwendolyn as your personal bodyguard. Her elven heritage allows her to stay awake for many turns of the clock so she could watch over you throughout the night. Your father is leaving, and you'll need all the help you can get. Gwendolyn will stay behind and give you whatever aid you may need."

Gwendolyn's face turned a bit red as Celedant added, "She can't speak because of a warlock's curse, but she can make herself understood."

"She seems to want to go with you, not stay here," the princess said.

Gwendolyn started to sign, but Goran stepped in.

"She'll stay by your side, no matter what," he said.

When Celedant turned to go, Gwendolyn grabbed him and gave him a deep kiss. The wizard's face blossomed into the brightest red.

"I will see you when this is all over," she signed.

Celedant did not say a word.

A day later the army prepared to ride to war. While the troops waited in the fields beyond the city, Haruldi prepared to take leave of Partha. He called his daughter into his chamber.

"As we discussed, you will stay and protect the people of Partha," he commanded. "Use your judgment to the best of your ability. If we fail, the city will be open to the forces of Zeiglon. If that happens, take as many as you can north to the dwarven realms. The wizard has promised us that the clans in the mountains will offer protection."

"But the city..." she asked, "what of it?"

Haruldi sighed. "The city could fall, sooner or later. The best way to save the people is to take them north. Await word on the battle. I will have messengers ready to bring you the news."

Haruldi kissed his daughter on the forehead.

He turned and left his chamber and took the stairs down to the yard. There he mounted his horse and a wave of his mailed hand started the company moving.

Haruldi and his knights rode at the head of his forces with Celedant, Goran and Azimuth bringing up the rear. The populace of the city turned out in droves to see Haruldi off to battle and they littered the streets with flowers for the company to ride over or passed flowers up to the knights as they rode down the streets. The soldiers used the colorful flowers to decorate their armor and their horses.

Goran looked over at the wizard. "Such fanfare for men who will likely be dead in a few days."

Celedant looked harshly at his friends. "Do you not have any hope?"

The dwarf shook his head. "Nope, nary a bit. Zeiglon can send many legions to die, but there is only a finite number of Parthians. Their losses will be keenly felt."

A general order was sent to all the foot soldiers who had been stationed around the grasslands to march north. While this infantry marched toward the forests of the north, they were ordered to force the evacuation of small towns and individual farms. When they reached the forested portion of Partha, they would then camp and await the news of the great battle that was to take place in the west.

Their orders were simple. If Partha then lost, they were to go north. There they would hope to rendezvous with Princes Eleanor and the fleeing citizens of the capital.

The Zeiglon army was camped in a slight valley with a shallow river running through it. King Zackery had ordered his main force to camp while the other units trickled in. Once they were all assembled, the army would attack Partha.

This was the invasion Zackery had been waiting for these many years.

Unbeknownst to the Zeiglon Army, Parthian scouts had discovered early on that their enemy's army occupied the valley, and they had sent word back to the king. They were keeping a close eye on the buildup of troops and were sending regular reports east to Haruldi.

The Parthian army was now riding ahead to trap their enemy before Zackery could assemble enough men to easily defeat them. The Parthian forces rode night and day in order to catch the Zeiglon army off guard and the latest reports from the Parthian scouts told them that the valley was now alight with enemy campfires.

Haruldi planned to attack one end of the valley while two prongs swept down on them from the sides. He sent the outriders to their positions and as the sun dawned, the main body of his horsemen crested the valley edge. They were utterly silent, with only the soft hoof beats and jingle of the tack of their horses to alert the forces of Zeiglon.

They then attacked in a great tide of horseflesh, shining sabers, and lances as they crashed into the foremost soldiers. Most were half asleep and still exiting their tents as the Parthian horses rode over them and devastated the front portion of the camp.

The blaring horns of the two prongs then crested the gentle rise and barreled down into the sides of the now alert camp. The Parthian forces cut deep into their enemy, easily slaughtering them, until the Zeiglon horns sounded from the south and west.

It had never occurred to the attackers that they would face only foot soldiers in the initial assault, and soon they did see the enemy's cavalry breaking cover and joining the battle. They, too, were only partially armored as they had been caught off guard. The Parthian scouts had never seen the horsemen vacate the camp under darkness of the previous night to seek better foraging areas, but thereby leave the valley filled with only infantry.

As the forces clashed, the southern portion of the Parthian army became trapped while futilely trying to fight their way across the camp. Realizing those troops were now pinned down, Haruldi called for the retreat to be trumpeted.

Suddenly a huge earthquake rolled through the continent and horses reared and men fell from their saddles. Footmen were tossed about like rag dolls as the ground undulated and horses turned to flee and bucked the steady hands that tried to keep them from all out panic.

The Parthian charge had broken, but now Haruldi's troops had to escape another disaster as the ground rumbled around them.

Zeiglon forces were undergoing the same upheaval. Their horses stumbled, dislodging their riders, and the soldiers on foot in the camp swayed back and forth in the waves of the ongoing earthquake. Suddenly the streamed split open and a huge fissure appeared and the earth poured into it. The soldiers of both armies were dragged down into its depths.

The remaining horsemen pulled hard on their reins to gain control of their mounts and they desperately began retreating from the battle.

Celedant had been riding beside Haruldi as the ground had begun to give way under their horse's hooves. Goran rode up and pulled at Celedant's horse's halter to turn the animal and rider away from the opening maw of the earth. Haruldi's horse faltered and its front hooves slid into the deep sand of the valley floor.

Celedant reached out and grasped Haruldi's armor just as his horse toppled over into the fissure. Goran's horse had pushed Celedant's to move away from certain death while the wizard held on to Haruldi's back plate. Its metal edge, though dull, cut into the wizard's hand as he attempted to pull the heavily armored man out of danger.

A second quake struck, and all their horses bucked and threatened to get away from them. Haruldi's back-plate, slick with blood from Celedant's hand, began sliding out from under the wizard's grip.

Haruldi reached around and shouted a command.

"Save yourself, wizard! This will be the death of us all."

He slapped Celedant's hand away and fell down into the sand and began rolling and flailing toward the fissure until he slowly disappeared into its depths.

CHAPTER TWENTY

After the many intentionally useless meetings between the two, the Zeiglon emperor, Zachary, again summoned Treakis to the castle. Zachary then clapped his hands in joy and ordered, "Someone go fetch the prince."

Several men-at-arms went and soon the prince stood in chains before the throne next to Treakis. Aedith and Treakis exchanged a slight nod of the head. Aedith was dressed in rags, but the emperor could see he was well muscled and, although pale and haggard with matted hair, he still appeared to be in good shape.

Treakis was the first to speak. "My own King and Queen will be pleased to see that their son has not been overly neglected."

Zachary smiled. "Yes. Royalty must stick together. However, all pleasantries aside, I must bring into question the treaty between your people and Partha. It disturbs me that you have dealings with our enemy."

"Those are just trade agreements, my lord," Treakis replied, waving away the emperor's concerns.

Zachary smiled, an evil look in his eyes.

"That may be so, but we need to present a warning to your people to show that dealing with the Parthians cannot be tolerated. So, for these transgressions, Prince Aedith will be executed."

There was a hushed awe about the room as the sentence was handed down. Prince Aedith struggled in his chains and the strength of the two guards holding his shackles was all that held him back.

The prince was led closer before the tyrant, his chains dragging across the stone floor, and as Zachary raised his staff to strike Aedith down, the elf pulled away from his guards and, despite his chains, lunged. He and the emperor struggled briefly before falling against the giant shell throne and toppling it backward. Myriad shells broke and slid across the marbled floor.

Aedith struggled and grappled with the emperor and grasped his staff of mithril while Zachary struggled to gain control of the Staff of Adois.

Suddenly, the courtiers saw a white light emanate from behind the throne. Aedith grasped the staff and the crystal flew from the floor where the emperor had dropped it and reattached itself to the length of mithril.

The Staff of Adaman had been remade.

The elven prince's chains then fell away into the dust and the combatants began to fight in earnest. As the two staves clashed against each other and the ground shook, great blocks of stone rained down upon the courtiers, and they ran screaming for the doors, fearful a final Armageddon had arrived.

Treakis ran toward his prince, but a sudden, great upheaval of the ground threw him to the floor. As the two combatants' staffs met, more bright white flashes of power erupted and caused the ground to rumble and ripple even more violently.

Treakis crawled over to the base of the throne and watched in fascination as the two combatants fought with their staffs while the world around them continued to disintegrate from the horrible, combined force of their staffs.

The crystals glowed with each strike as their power was unleashed. The whole building was now rocking and soon the walls and towers toppled. The back wall of the room fell away and Treakis saw towering spires of land slowly pushing out of the sea while the remaining, flat slabs of the land fell into the churning ocean.

All around him was destruction. One of the greatest cities in the known world was being demolished with unbelievable violence. People fled their homes as their houses fell down around them. Most of the inhabitants could not reach safety and they became trapped in the eddy of the destruction of the city around them.

Clouds of smoke began to rise as fires ravished great portions of the city, and continuing quakes opened fissures in the ground which swallowed whole sections of the buildings and land.

Meanwhile the prince and the king battled. The staff of Adaman blazed white in the glory of good. The staff of Adois flamed blood red for its forces of evil.

With each strike of a staff, the power of the forces injured each of the two fighters. The flashes of fire burned away flesh and opened deep wounds on each combatant while the unleashed power of the staffs laid waste to the land about them.

The city was in ruins and its citizens were trapped, dead or dying. The land itself rose with each quake, and the sea fell ever deeper, far below the emperor's throne room.

One more great blast ensued as the two staffs clashed together one final time, and such a great force erupted from them that Treakis was bowled over. He rolled like a ragdoll to the throne room's wall, the remaining stone wobbled and fell, and Treakis was trapped beneath the rubble.

After many clicks of the clock, Treakis was finally able to free himself from the rubble. He brushed himself off, looked around, and found nothing but death.

He had only survived the final cataclysm of destruction because he had been covered by the great stones from the wall.

He stumbled out across the room as another quake shuttered through the capital and threw him to the ground again.

"My Prince, where are you?" he called out.

Treakis heard a great, slow hissing and saw that the throne room had now been moved near the precipice of a cliff that went down hundreds of rods to the ocean below. The hissing had come from lava that had flowed out from the cliff's face and had been landing down in the cool waters of the sea below.

Treakis heard moaning.

He followed the sounds and came to the throne that was also now on the edge of the cliff. Another quake shook the area and he watched as the land spires reared up even further out of the sea.

Then he saw what was left of his prince.

Aedith's body was a mass of charred flesh, bearing little resemblance to an elf. The prince still grasped his staff tightly in hands that looked more like the skeletal claws of a nightmarish beast. His broken body was wrapped around the staff of mithril, adorned with its many facetted gem.

Treakis rushed over and dropped to his knees, fearful to touch his prince. The body before him was so pale and so broken, but Treakis would have recognized his boyhood friend anywhere even though underneath its charred skin.

The prince held the staff flat against his body and with open, unseeing eyes stared out to the sea.

When a raspy voice issued forth from the broken body before him, Treakis was astonished,

"The staff saved me," it said, "but only for a while. Who is it there?"

The emissary whispered, "Treakis, my lord."

The prince looked toward him with his sightless eyes, and his smile brought a bloody trickle down the prince's burned chin.

"Dear Treakis...that we should meet so. I have little time. Lord Zachary and I fought, and this staff, the Staff of Adaman, was remade. As it was transformed, a great power was unleashed because of the evil in his staff, the Staff of Adois, and the evil that Zachary held within himself. The Staff of Adaman flew from his hands into mine and a great energy washed over us, throwing us to the walls and floor. Outside the building, the energy exploded and the building shook, but remained standing. At least that is what I perceived."

The prince had a fit of coughing that brought up bright blood.

"I am dying. Quickly. Take the staff, pry off the gem, and throw the staff into the sea. I can hear waves nearby. You must take the gem to our homeland. The elders will know what to do with it. The staff is too powerful to remain whole. Zachary has used the pieces for too many evil deeds. It must be cleansed by time before it can be remade."

"My lord, the rear of the palace has fallen into the sea," Treakis said. "Where once the ground sloped downward, high cliffs have risen. I shall cast the staff down them into the crashing sea and I will then take the gem back home with me," he promised his lord.

There was another great rending of the continent, and they could see that the ground had risen again. A wall toppled, and the prince moaned in pain.

"Quickly now, my friend, do my bidding," he said in between the stabs of pain.

Treakis took his dagger and pried off the headpiece from the staff. Laying the gem beside the prince, he stood on shaky legs and made his way to the cliff's edge. The stone on which the palace had been built was sheared away, and the castle floor was now several hundred rods in the air. Around it, where once there had been ground, a wild undulating sea crashed against the ruins.

Treakis took the staff and hurled it like a javelin with all his might out into the roiling ocean. He returned to Aedith, but too late to tell his prince that his wish had been accomplished. The prince had died.

The guards that Treakis had brought with him stumbled through the debris. Treakis had the soldiers take a tapestry down from the wall and gently roll the broken body of the prince into it.

Treakis found a satchel in the dust on the floor and emptied it of the now useless messages that had been destined for the court of Zeiglon. He took the gem and placed it inside.

He and the remaining elves took up the prince's body and began the arduous walk out of the ruined city.

CHAPTER TWENTY-ONE

T reakis' guards had refused to stay in the city itself because of what had happened to the last elven contingent that had come to Zeiglon. They had chosen to camp instead in the high woods surrounding the metropolis.

They were therefore miles from the capital of Zeiglon when the hot air began to wash over them and the soldiers had to hold tight to their horse's reins and tethering ropes. They watched as trees and boulders suddenly whipped through the air like small playthings. One tree tore a bloody swath through their contingent, killing several of the elves, and then came the explosive boom that caused the real damage. The immense "kaboom" was louder than any noise they had ever heard and many clapped their hands over their ears in a feeble attempt to escape it.

Behind them their horses reared in terror and most of them bolted in equine madness, white froth spilling from their mouths. The elves tried to hold onto the other panicky horses, but these mounts too reared up and were gone, more powerful in their fear than an elf could hang on to.

The boom had lasted for what seemed like forever—although it was no more than a few ticks of the clock - and then the wind from the blast subsided and the elves began to collect themselves.

Their captain ordered several to stay with the dead and sent a group of two to look for their mounts. He took the rest on foot at a fast run toward the city. As they neared the capital, the trees showed more and more damage. First they saw that the leaves had been stripped away and then the branches were gone, too. As they moved further on, they discovered that the entire forest of trees that had surrounded the city had been knocked down, blown over by the high winds.

When the elves reached the outer city, they saw the once gleaming houses and businesses were now in utter ruin and as they walked, they had to dodge the walls of several buildings as they fell apart or collapsed. Survivors were struggling to climb from the rubble. Many called out for help, but the elves kept moving onward, their goal much more important, they thought, than trying to help the citizens of Zeiglon.

Every now and then the ground shook again and if it were not for the elves' keen balance, they would have fallen over, just like the trees.

The great wall that had once protected the inner city lay in ruin after being blasted outward and flattening the nearby houses. The elves picked their way through the rubble and finally reached the city center. The once vibrant metropolis was horrendously damaged. Not a single complete structure could be seen. What remained were slender walls or chimneys that stuck up straight from the ground, like skeletal bones reaching for the sky.

Several new quakes, even more violent than before, struck and the ground rolled and heaved. The elves were thrown down to the ground and several were injured. In some places red liquid stone began pouring forth and the lava pooled within the destroyed city. The elves stood and now could see that ahead of them, over the flattened dwellings, only a portion of the palace remained standing.

As they walked, the continuous shaking, rising and falling of the ground made their footing ever more dangerous. They slowed their pace, dodging lava as it pooled about the destroyed buildings and ate into the tumbled stone or cooled in white-hot patches. Moving as carefully as they could, they continued through the destruction until they neared the only thing left standing…the palace.

They had not seen a living being for some time now, but found only an occasional pulped body, hardly recognizable as a once living thing. The landscape was bare except for the foundations of the buildings that had surrounded the palace.

The elves neared the royal structure, which stood oddly erect and undamaged amid the devastation, at least the part visible to them. The windows and doors had been blown outward, but the front of the building was sound. Ever watchful the elves kept their swords drawn, not knowing what kind of sorcery had been released to cause such a force.

Inside, they found the shadows of bodies, incinerated against walls, all blown from one central location.

As they neared the throne room, which appeared to be the area where the explosion had originated, they stared at the base of the shelled throne of Zeiglon. They were shocked to see clear sky above them and to hear the sound of crashing waves beyond the fallen rear walls. Even as they stood at the entrance of the hall, the ground shuddered once more, and they were thrown down against the marble floor.

They righted themselves and heard a horrible grinding sound. Another section of the palace wall had slipped downward and crashed into the sea below. They knew that Zeiglon had once held a harbor, but it had disappeared, and the rocks it had been built upon had risen into the high cliffs that now ringed the rear of the palace.

Turning away from the sight of the devastation all around him, the elven captain finally spotted what they had all been looking for. Lord Treakis kneeled in front of them, holding the remains of the prince.

CHAPTER TWENTY-TWO

Goran and Celedant's horses began making head way through the thick sand and before long they were atop what had recently been a small stream-fed valley. Azimuth was waiting for them.

He had felt the earth begin to rumble and stopped at the edge of the valley, but he was unable to call his friends back. He had tried telepathy with Celedant, but the wizard was already fighting his horse to get to safety. Now all that remained in front of Celedant and Goran was a waterfall where the fissure had opened and claimed all of the valley.

It did not matter whose side any soldier had been on. All were fleeing the disaster.

After they had met up, Azimuth, Goran and Celedant were soon recognized by the Parthian horsemen as companions of King Haruldi, and his cavalry swarmed toward them. When the wizard saw what was occurring, he rose in his saddle and motioned those riders to the east and away from danger. Another quake struck, though, felling the riders and horses alike.

Eventually the remnants of the Parthian horsemen were streaming their way to the east, their horse's eyes wild with fright.

The Parthian army had been decimated first by the rear attacks of the Zeiglon cavalry, and then by the fissure that had opened with the quakes. The ground had opened up, swallowing most of them, along with most of the foot soldiers of the Zeiglon army. The others who were in the valley were lucky to escape with their lives.

Then, after a moment of silence, the battle continued and the Zeiglon horsemen pursued the retreating Parthians. Ever so often, Celedant would turn in his saddle and cast a spell at the army following him, but he had little effect on such a large force.

Aware of the nearing danger, Azimuth telepathically called over to Celedant, *I'm going to ride behind one of these small rises and morph into my dragon form. We'll see if I can't slow them down.*

The wizard did not even question his friend's plan.

Azimuth separated from the Parthian Calvary and quickly became hidden in a small gully that suited his purpose exactly. He dismounted and staked down his horse, hopeful it would not be scared away when he changed. Then Azimuth lay down as far away from the horse as he could and spoke the words that would change him into a dragon.

A multicolored swirl covered him and suddenly he had changed. His golden scales sparkled in the sunlight. With two flaps of his wings and a massive shove off the ground he was aloft and quickly gaining height.

Azimuth cruised over the mass of horses below and dove down on to the Zeiglon horseman. As he passed the front ranks, he let loose his fiery breath and incinerated many of their horsemen. He turned in a semicircle and flew back through the middle of the horsemen once again and let loose his powerful blast of fire.

He felt sorry for the horses that he killed, but he knew he needed to get the Parthians to safety.

On the ground, the leaders of the Zeiglon horsemen were killed on Azimuth's first fiery pass. The men that followed them halted as quickly as they could, their horses in a panic. Many shot arrows into the air at the dragon, but their feathered missiles merely bounced off the thick scales of the flying dragon.

Many of the cavalry began calling out "Dragon!" and turned away from the chase, but Azimuth flew after them spewing forth fire just to ensure they remained no threat.

The Parthians heard the screams of the Zeiglon men and the panic of their horses and slowed to look back at their pursuers. The Parthians were flabbergasted to see a golden dragon burning its way through their enemies and many called out that the gods had sent the beast for their safety.

Celedant knew better and watched, in amazement himself, as Azimuth slowly winged his way over the Zeiglon force. He was startled how Azimuth made the flight look so effortless and glided so easily in and out of the horsemen.

The Zeiglon forces had had enough and they began riding hard back the way they had come. The Parthians raised their weapons and cheered at their retreating enemies. Many of them grasped holy sigils and thanked their gods for the deliverance of the dragon.

Finally, Azimuth had had enough killing for the day and he dove low to the ground and landed in the ravine where his flight had begun. He immediately changed forms and found his horse, gently eating away at the thick grass. Mounting up, he quickly rejoined the Parthian ranks and made his way to the head of the column looking for Celedant.

He called forth telepathically, *Celedant where are you?*

The wizard told him and soon Azimuth was riding beside Goran and Celedant. The dragon spoke out loud to Celedant.

"Well, what do you think, my friend?"

Celedant spoke silently back to his friend, *It was magnificent. Never have I seen you fly in such a way. But weren't you afraid of revealing yourself?*

Not really. In the battle the soldiers had little time to grasp the difference between a dragon and a firedrake. They might have called me a dragon, but to them I was a mere firedrake. Besides, it was a chance I had to take. Otherwise we would have been overrun by the end of the day. Despite the carnage I was a part of, I at least slowed them down enough so we could get away.

The Parthians began to pull away from the battleground and Celedant and Goran took the lead of the cavalry, comfortable now that they were going to survive this day.

The wizard looked around him. Barely a third of the force that had been set out was still following him. Their pursuers had broken off the chase after the dragon attack, thus allowing the Parthians to slow and rest their horses.

The ground still trembled, but the horses were exhausted and barely reacted to the still undulating land.

Continuing back to the capital at a slower pace, Celedant called for the surviving captains. Several came in heed of his command and he looked at the bloodied men.

"King Haruldi was swallowed up by the fissure," he informed them. "His daughter now rules the city and the nation until we can locate her brother. We must get to the city as soon as possible. We will alternate between resting the horses and riding them toward the capital. The clerics can see to the wounded when we walk the horses. Should the enemy be ordered forward again, we must be ready to ride at a moment's notice." He paused and continued. "Send out scouts. We will walk for the next turn of the clock. Water the horses with what you have, and then let's move on."

They rode and passed several streams, all flooding their banks. They stopped often to refresh their horses and eventually reached the great bridge over the river. It too was flooded and its supports had cracked from the earthquakes. Beyond, the fields were flooded as well.

The further they went, the higher the water rose. It wasn't long before the horses were in deep water that covered the riders' boots. Celedant turned them north toward higher ground. Reaching an area where the flooding was not as deep, the army turned and galloped in great sprays of water as best they could as they continued to the north. They were still unable, though, to find a sure way through the ever-deepening water to proceed further east.

Once they reached the foothills, they could turn east, but deep water was still present. Celedant had no explanation for the quakes, but they continued as they threaded through downed trees and newly created mounds of dirt and rock in the wooded hills.

When night fell, the army camped in the forested hills where the wounded could be better served by the clerics and healers.

In the morning the waters looked to have crested, but as far as the eye could see there was nothing but dirty brown flood water. The horses would not drink it, and the men found it too briny. Celedant stood looking out over the flooded lands.

"What could have done this?" Goran asked him.

"It felt as if the ground dropped further with each successive quake," Azimuth said. "If so, the sea has come to reclaim the land."

"Something powerful and magical caused those quakes," Celedant said and shook his head sadly. "I fear that Partha is no more. May we hope that Zeiglon experienced the same fate? I mourn for Haruldi. I knew him for only a short time and found him to be brave, fair and just."

Treakis and his escort of elven warriors walked through the rubble that had been Zeiglon. All the while deep rumblings could still be heard, and at times the ground shifted beneath their feet. The elves' keen senses could also feel the ground moving ever so slowly upward. They could make better time once they left the city, even though they still carried their prince's body.

When they reached the point in the forest where their party had divided during battle, they found that several of the soldiers were still missing. Treakis' party managed to corral six horses, but then they waited for several turns of the clock as more soldiers trickled back with two more horses. Meanwhile the elves had ranged out and found various roots and plants to carry out a makeshift embalming of the prince's body.

Treakis and several of the soldiers who had served with the prince openly wept as they tended to the broken body. Preservative leaves were first packed tightly about Aedith and then they sewed the tapestry tight around his body and secured the prince onto one of the horses. It was dark before they were ready to go.

Carefully they led the horses down the tree and limb strewn road westward.

The next day the road ended abruptly. They had reached the edge of the destruction during the night, and they could make better time jogging beside the horses, but as the sun had risen, the road ended. Dark clouds greeted them, and a sheer cliff wall fell away from the road. Below they could see only dense fog covering the ground for mile upon mile.

They camped by the road, not knowing exactly what had happened there, and they waited to see how best to proceed. Over the next two days a westerly wind eventually blew the fog away, revealing yet again destruction beyond belief. When the land had shifted, the ocean had rushed in and submerged the area below the cliffs and salted the entire land, turning it into a future desert.

A shallow surface of briny water ran as far as the eye could see, a giant lake of seawater they were trapped behind. The rivers were all flooded with brackish water and were now unable to flow east to the ocean anymore. Water lay in front of them, stagnate and unusable to any living thing.

The water had apparently rushed over the trees in one giant wall and had destroyed everything in its path. Now the flotsam stretched ever westward beyond their eyesight. Below them, an empty plain was dotted here and there by tree stumps that had somehow refused to be wrenched up out of the ground by the flood of water.

The elves stood there dumfounded.

Treakis puzzled over the problem of descending hundreds of spans down to the new floor of the land below. The cliff was sharply cut, and there was little dirt or rock accumulated at its bottom. Most of it had been carried away by the flood. They had no choice but to find a way down the cliff in order to continue north to their homeland.

They let the horses go and began tying ropes together. When finished, they tied the long cord to a tree and lowered it, but it was three rods short of the bottom. Several sure handed elves quickly climbed down and then the prince was lowered. Soon they were all at the bottom, packing up what food and water they had.

The elves began a soggy, loping run that slowly ate up the miles. Although they could go long periods of time without rest, they still needed to eat. Soon their rations and water ran out, even before they had reached or even sighted the foothills of the Mordolwyn mountains.

The submerged land now gave way to the grass lands of Partha, but all they found were burned out homesteads. They stopped and camped for the night at one of the houses.

All day long a hot arid wind had been blowing from the west Treakis recognized that as one more anomaly because it was spring and usually that meant rain, instead of a dry wind from the southern mountains.

His scouts had also seen a column of soldiers moving north toward them along the trail. As the elves ran onward, the horsemen followed and the elves realized they could not outrun their pursuers who they now knew were mounted. As they closed in on the elves, it became obvious that they were Zeiglon horsemen.

When the elves had passed through Partha, they had heard a rumor that Zeiglon had invaded, although they had seen no sign of it. Those kinds of rumors had been flying about for decades, but now they realized that at the very least a raiding party was behind them. The Zeiglon soldiers would not care a whit about killing elves or about the fact that they carried the body of their dead prince.

The elven officer motioned Treakis who fell in and ran along beside him. Without showing any sign of the days he'd spent running, the officer spoke easily despite his steady gait.

"My Lord, those horsemen will overtake us in a day. There is no way we can withstand them. Take the prince's body and hide till they are past. Then continue north. My soldiers and I will lead them a merry chase and make a stand far from here. We may see you in Ravannhiel someday, but I think not. The prince must be returned to his homeland."

Treakis nodded. He knew the officer was correct. The prince had to be returned, not just his body, but the head piece of the Staff of Adaman also had to be kept safe. Without a word Treakis raced up the rocky expanse away from his countrymen and found a covered overhang to hide in. The elves stopped to hide Treakis' escape, but once he was hidden, they took off running again and headed northwest.

Half a day later, Treakis heard the thunder of hooves as the forces of Zeiglon passed his hiding place and continued to chase after the elves.

That afternoon the elven commander stopped at the edge of some foothills and called out to the troops.

"If you see a place to make a stand, call out. The riders will be upon us as the sun crests the eastern sky."

Soon a scout returned and, still on the run, reported, "There is an outcropping of sandstone ahead that offers a good defensive position."

The elves peeled off from their current course and followed the scout to the sandstone layers of rock he had found. There were small, eroded cave-like positions that offered ledges overhead to block arrows and solid ground underneath to lie on.

Their commander spoke to them all.

"We have drawn the enemy away from Lord Treakis and our prince. We can only hope they will make it back to Ravannhiel safely. Now, pick your positions well. Save your arrows for sure shots, and we may yet survive."

The elves quickly picked out the places that offered the best protection and they took up their positions on the rocky ground. The commander and several elves built a rock wall along the top of the outcropping so those elves could see the battle better and relay information to the commander.

The defenders took what time they had to rest and even sleep a little. The long run had been taxing, even for the stoic elven soldiers.

As the sun rose the next morning, the Zeiglon cavalry was nearly onto their position. Their scouts were out in front of the column following the faint trail the elves had left in the rocky soil.

The elf next to the commander leaned over and whispered to him, "They are coming straight at us. The horsemen know we're here."

"Yes," his superior agreed. "We must prepare to call to the others to hold their fire until the horsemen get close. I will draw them in and then let fly."

The Zeiglon scouts drew closer and closer to the rocky outcropping. The elven commander stood up with an arrow notched that he let fly. The projectile arced into the air, and the first scout pitched back off his saddle. He followed this with another arrow that took a second scout in the throat. The next pitched off his horse with an arrow sticking in one eye.

The Zeiglon cavalry broke into a charge, and the other elves let fly their arrows. More horsemen were knocked off their steeds, dead or dying. The other horsemen drew their short bows and fired back but most of their arrows broke upon the stone face of the elven defense.

One elf, just in the process of firing his arrow, was struck and he pitched forward to the ground below. Then a cat and mouse game of attrition began.

The cavalry dismounted and picked out where the arrows were coming from. They waited until one elf rose to shoot at them and the men in that section all shot at once, their arrows rattling off the sandstone and bringing down that elven soldier.

The elves fought on from their protected hiding places, but their soldiers suffered horribly.

The commander of the Zeiglon forces had held back some forty odd soldiers and those were now led forward. They rode hard for the rear of the escarpment and once past the onslaught of elven arrows, they dismounted and began the long climb toward the elven commander's stronghold.

The elves fired at the advancing men once they had crested the rear hill, but the men returned their fire viciously, and first one, then another of the elves fell. The commander himself collected what was left of their arrows, shot back and dropped man after man to the stony soil.

When they were within ten rods of his position, he drew his sword and dove into the advancing troops.

As he rolled into the middle of the attackers, his first two swings were true, and two men fell dead. He began parrying and thrusting, dropping the enemy left and right. He had been fighting since Zeiglon had only been a small fishing village, and his battle skills spoke of this truth.

Suddenly a sword took him in the back and punctured his lung. Frothy blood rolled down his chin, but he still fought on. He killed three more of his enemy before the Zeiglon captain stepped up behind the weakened elf and in a one swing decapitated him.

The horsemen began climbing the eroded sandstone to get to the rest of the entrenched elves. At each defensive position, the sheer numbers of the humans slowly wore the elves down, but not without many men being pushed off the escarpment or bearing horrific wounds.

It took the better part of the day for the humans to search out each and every elf, but in the end, they cleared the escarpment. That night the Zeiglon men slept the sleep of the dead as they camped on the top of the rock formation.

They were up before dawn, and the captain motioned toward the dead that lay all about.

"We don't have the time to bury them," he said. "We'd be here more than half the day, picking through this rocky soil, and besides, we don't have enough food and water to last us much longer. We have horse meat aplenty, but lack of water will kill us all the same. Leave the bodies, but search the dead for extra food and water. I want to be gone from this place of death within a turn of the clock."

In the end there were only forty-two of his men who mounted up to move on. They left the better part of a hundred of their dead companions behind in the dusty, rocky soil.

Treakis had waited until dark. Using his elven eyesight, he had watched the horsemen gallop past before he headed northward. His food and water had run out before he entered the forest below the foothills. Despite his elven endurance, the ambassador had reached his limit. His legs and hands were bloody from falling numerous times, and the prince's body weighed heavily on his shoulders.

Treakis had to live off the land, surviving on fish and crawfish from small streams, and snaring animals when he reached the foothills proper.

He began to follow a riverbed that generally led north. The water kept him going, even though the body of his prince weighed heavily on both his strength and his soul. As he made his way up alongside the river, his elven hearing picked up on several people trying to silently approach him from the brush.

Casually he lay his prince down on the ground just as four orcs emerged from the tree lined bank.

Seeing he was just a lone elf, they charged. Treakis had his sword out immediately and he jumped towards the orcs. He cut one down, immediately severing its neck, and the remaining orcs came at him from either side. One of them thrust his sword at Treakis, but the elf just moved out of the way. He reached out and grasped the orc's forearm and gave it a strong pull. As that orc fell, Treakis parried the last orc's attack and neatly stabbed the orc. It fell to the ground.

He then faced one alone. The last was more skilled than the others and he feinted low and then flipped up his blade into the air, trying for Treakis' throat.

Treakis dodged the sword, but fell over backwards. He felt an intense pain and at once knew that his leg had been broken. Treakis lay in the ravine and took his sword and threw it at the orc.

The sword whipped through the air and struck the orc in the chest. He slowly settled to the ground.

For several turns of the clock Treakis lay there. He knew his leg was broken. All of a sudden, his journey had become much harder. He found a branch and some vines to splint his leg while pondering what to do next.

Finally, he started pulling the prince's body upward and crawling with it as best he could. The pain was unending and beyond any he had ever endured.

Soon he heard voices calling to one another, no doubt as they followed the tracks of his dragging leg, he thought,. He panicked, but then relaxed slightly when he heard a gravelly voice.

"Donna move another inch, elf."

Treakis looked ahead and somewhat to his relief saw that it was not a Zeiglon soldier, but a dwarf with a blond beard. Next he was surrounded by ten dwarves, and he could tell that by his armor and charisma, the first, blond bearded dwarf was their leader. He wore dull, but well-made chain mail and carried a well-polished double headed axe. He knelt down before Treakis and spoke.

"I am Yorgi of the clan Yorgi. What brings an elf to our doorstep?"

Treakis looked into the depths of the dwarf's eyes and saw nothing but wisdom and intelligence. Wiping the dirt from his face, he responded, "I am Treakis, representative of Ravannhiel to the Zeiglon court."

The dwarf spat. "Do not mention that name, elf. Tell me this. Was it your race that brought on these earthquakes? My people have suffered greatly."

"No. It was the emperor of Zeiglon and a powerful relic that he yielded," Treakis replied.

"Humph. If it had been ye, I'd killed ye on the spot. Now it seems I am bound to help ye. But in these times, as the earth keeps heaving, many of me people are dead or trapped. Those who survived are camping in the cold open air. I am bound to ask ye for a token for our help. What do you carry in that bag ye so importantly drag behind ye?"

"It is the body of my Prince. The emperor murdered him, so I carry his remains to Ravannhiel to rest with his kindred."

There were several gasps by the dwarves as they grasped the religious symbols that had appeared from their pockets.

Yorgi too looked sternly at the elf.

"Tis a noble deed ye are attempting. But ye'll never reach yer homeland without help." He thought for a moment. "Tending to yer leg will cost our already depleted clerics precious time as they tend to our own. What can ye give to me clan as payment for such help? Me clans' plight is terrible, and I'd sooner leave ye to die here as my own kin are in such dire straits."

Treakis had only one thing to bargain for his life with these greedy dwarves. At the same time he realized that they could just kill him and take his possessions. He knew there was no love lost between the two races. But what choice did he have? Opening up the satchel at his side, he drew forth the head piece to the staff of Adaman.

The dwarves to a soul fell silent. One whispered, "Kill him now and take the jewel."

Yorgi held his hand up. "No, we'd be none better than a stinking orc if we did that. Elf, ye freely would give that to me for our aid?"

Treakis nodded. "I have nothing else, and the need is pressing."

Yorgi reverently took the jewel, which was a bit too large for his callused hand. He whispered to the others, "We take the elf and his prince to our lands. He is under me protection and should any harm come to him, ye will answer to me."

Treakis was hauled up none too gently by one dwarf, and they all began the trek to Yorgi's clan.

Treakis arranged for the dwarves to keep the prince's body in a deep stone tomb while he waited for the elves to come retrieve it. Treakis' leg was healing and had been properly splinted for support. His therapy was accompanied by dwarvan healing spells and he was ready to travel after a month. Yorgi gave him a mountain horse to speed his journey onwards.

Through the next weeks he rode towards Ravannhiel, but a deep mist lay over the forest and the fog kept him from seeing his homeland. He did not know until he passed through the river Ammoniel that he was finally in the land of his birth.

There was still a mist there, too, and it covered everything. As he neared his beloved trees of Ravannhiel, he was hailed.

"Who advances?"

"I am Treakis, emissary for the royal house."

He was allowed forward, but oddly enough, it seemed to him, he was immediately surrounded by his kindred. Endless questions were shouted at him. That struck him as terribly strange for such a noble folk as this.

Then he noticed the dirt and debris that covered their bodies.

"What goes on here?" he shouted above their barrage of questions.

One soldier hushed the crowd and started his tale.

"The ground moved in great quakes, and large fissures opened throughout our lands. Then the North Sea rushed in." There tears came into his eyes. "The ground began falling and many cities were destroyed by the quakes. The ground lowered and lowered and the sea slowly began eating away at our kingdom. Our mages could do little. Our people ran before the incoming water. With each quake, the land dipped lower and the water rose more steadily. Most of our folk escaped, but many stayed in their tree top homes. We know not what happened to them, but we fear the worst. The sea came quicker and quicker and we ran before its high waves. Many of us were overcome, but most escaped to the east. I do not know about the lands to the west. Now it is estimated that tens of thousands of square acres of our homeland lie underwater. As you know, the ground has quieted and the sea has stopped its encroachment, but mostly we are homeless and living on the forest floor. We all wait with foreboding whatever will come next."

Treakis hung his head in sorrow. His home had been in the north, along the coast, and it too had to be under the sea now. And what had happened to his family?

CHAPTER TWENTY-THREE

Celedant and his friends made their way to the front of the horsemen, where the remaining King's captains were organizing the retreat both from the Zeiglon forces and from the rising water. The commanders welcomed Celedant and one came up to him to ride beside the renowned wizard. He introduced himself.

"I am presently the highest-ranking officer, Lord Friedel, and I've just caught up with what is left of the army. I hope you can offer us as good advice as you did to our King. I fear he did not live through the ambush and subsequent quakes."

"Alas, the king fell in the valley," Celedant agreed. "I am sorry for his loss, but we cannot mourn at this time. The water is rising still."

"Yes," agreed the commander. "There's also the fact that a sizable force of Zeiglon horsemen is paralleling us as they try to escape the water, too."

"Have they offered battle yet?" Goran asked.

"Nay, master dwarf," Friedel replied. "They ride north as we do and keep their distance."

Could it be because they, too, no longer have a home to return to, Celedant wondered?

Once we settle in for the night, I'll fly over the area and assess the damage, Azimuth told the wizard telepathically.

Good idea, Celedant thought back.

Aloud he said, "The plan was to evacuate the city and go north into the mountains to escape an eventual siege, but these quakes and this rising water have already started that. With luck, I hope we will find the citizens safely ensconced in the foothills."

Friedel nodded. "I too hope we do. But with so many Zeiglon horsemen nearby, I fear they will attack once we do reach firmer ground."

At that moment a scout rode splashed up to them, panting after his difficult ride.

"The enemy has shifted direction and is riding hard to intercept us," he reported.

The trumpets sounded and orders were issued. The army would go forth to attack, while the wounded and those on foot would be escorted ahead. The mounted army turned and started riding slowly. With luck, they would fall in upon the rear of the Zeiglon horsemen.

They turned northwest in ankle deep water and began a slow advance. They dared not go faster for fear of riding into a stream bed or a hole and breaking their horse's legs.

Before long, the scouts returned with the news that the rear of the enemy's column had been sighted. The Parthian commanders conferred and they turned more to the north.

Soon the Zeiglon riders were spotted. Friedel rose up in his saddle and dropped his hand to signal the column to break into separate formations of horsemen, one hundred rods across. They began a slow trot, but as they grew nearer to the enemy, their pace increased.

The Zeiglon cavalry spotted the danger from behind and tried to form up to counterattack, but they were too slow and too late.

The Parthians crashed into their column and a thunderous clash ensued as the horsemen engaged each other while briny, muddy water was kicked up by their mounts. The Parthians formation that was not part of the first attack struck the Zeiglon riders further up the line.

Celedant was in the first rank to strike the enemies. Dragon Bolt was released, and the wizard was again surprised at what it could do. He swung it with ease and cut through enemy shields and armor alike. The sword was light as a feather, and Zeiglon horsemen fell left and right in front of him.

As soon as he had passed through their ranks, he turned his horse and charged back into the fray. As he rode through the enemy horsemen again, Dragon Bolt continued to rise and fall. Nothing could withstand its magic.

Suddenly a horn sounded, and the head of the Zeiglon column turned and charged back to its rear. Celedant raised his staff, calling on the power of both the ground and the water, and sent a massive wave of muddied water rushing at the oncoming riders. The water rose and crested at twenty cubits and broke as it reached the charging horsemen. The force threw many riders backward off their horses, and they were then ridden over by the second rank as they too plunged into the water's surge.

Celedant followed with a lightning spell that arched across the ground and struck in the midst of the other riders. The initial strike killed all within a twenty-foot range and its electricity ran through the water, shocking the horses and causing them to buck off their riders. The charge was brought to a standstill.

Into this now confused and demoralized mass of soldiers the Parthians charged. Their swords were held out like lances and they swung in wide arcs, cutting left and right. War horses slammed against each other's chests with loud wet thumps, and they reared up on their hind legs and flailed in the air, their riders clinging on for dear life.

Celedant was again in the mix. He had lost sight of both Goran and Azimuth, so he allowed his horse to take him where it would. His sword arm was bloodied due to Dragon Bolt's effectiveness in wounding the enemy, and he continued swinging right and left, never tiring. Once he was in the clear again, he saw that the Parthian horsemen had mixed their ranks and the captains were busy trying to straighten them out. The wounded were being led away to a small hillock that was still above water and there were dead horses and men spread across the fields, floating obscenely, half under the water.

The Zeiglon horsemen who had ridden out of the battle mustered to the north of the Parthians and addressed their lines in preparation for a massed charge. Friedel appeared from nowhere, a bloody bandage around his upper right arm, and formed up the Parthians.

They straightened into a proper unified formation just as their enemies charged.

Celedant sent lightning bolt after lightning bolt into the massed charge, but despite the number killed, it barely slowed the Zeiglon army down.

Friedel and his Parthians charged. They were outnumbered and bloodied, but took the charge to heart, laying aside their fears as they charged into the stronger Zeiglon forces. The sides met in another thunderous clash, but not nearly as forceful as earlier as their horses were beginning to tire.

Zeiglon forces overlapped the Parthians and had almost surrounded them, but the Parthians were pushing through their enemies by sheer force of will. To fall from a horse was to die, the crushing of body against body was so tight. Dead men were still mounted because there was no room for the bodies to fall.

Finally the lead Parthians pushed through the Zeiglon cavalry and looked back to see a swath of rider-less horses, some limping, others laying still in the water. Men of both sides walked knee deep in the churned ground. Some helped others and some were in a complete daze. The two sides of the Zeiglon cavalry had broken apart and ridden off to the west, leaving the Parthians in control of the battlefield.

Celedant was breathless and appalled. He had never been through such a trial. He looked up and saw both Goran and Azimuth making their way over to him, both with wild smiles on their faces, happy to be alive.

The Parthians collected their wounded and continued north, leaving Zeiglon's wounded on the small hillock. They met up with their own wounded and those without horses who they had sent ahead. All continued north and they were soon in the foothills and out of the water.

The riders from Zeiglon had not all given up yet, and they continued to follow the fleeing Parthian horsemen.

CHAPTER TWENTY-FOUR

When the first quake hit Partha, it had disintegrated much of the city. Many of the granite block buildings were toppled, many roofs caved in, and the water had risen up over the docks. The ships in port cut their ropes as they rose with the water, but that did not save them. The vessels crashed into the city's warehouses as the waves swept them inland instead of out to sea. Those unlucky enough to be without a quick-witted captain or first mate toppled over on their sides and were pulled under water by the mooring lines tied to the docks.

The fast-rising water was everywhere, and many citizens were trapped or had disappeared under the violent crashing waves, never to be seen again. In the city, people had watched, dumbstruck, as the water crept up the hills and submerged neighborhoods as it went. Eventually it stopped rising, but out on the plain, the deep water continued past the hills and threatened to surround the city.

The king's daughter, Princess Eleanor, had acted quickly and had ordered the guard to evacuate the city to the higher ground in the north. Unfortunately, as she issued the order, another quake hit, and the ground shifted again and the princess felt it drop.

Out in the streets, many of the populace tried to escape the city and its toppling buildings. Others stood dumfounded and stared at the destruction around them. The first refugees from the city stampeded out of the north gate as the guards tried to move them along in some semblance of order, but they found it was difficult to keep the people calm as the brown, debris laden seawater encroached ever closer.

Eleanor had the most precious of Partha's treasures crammed into a carriage. She mounted her horse while the house cavalry awaited her orders. Next to her Gwendolyn too was mounted. She signed frantically to the princess, pointing at the gate, and then leaned out and grabbed the reins of the royal horse, trying to pull it toward the gate

She felt a sword tap her on the shoulder.

"Let go of the princess or I'll put you down," one of the royal guards told her grimly.

Gwendolyn realized she had no choice and consigned herself to waiting for Eleanor.

The princess knew it would take many turns of the clock for the city to empty and if she were seen fleeing, it would set the population into a greater state of panic. Even though she herself was panicky, her father had always preached self-control…but he had never had a city falling down around him, she knew.

The guard captain came up to her and bowed.

"Your Royal Highness, the streets are going to be blocked soon. We must leave."

"No. I shall stay until the last click of the clock," she replied calmly. "Take the wagon and half your men. Go seek safety in the northern highlands."

As if to emphasis her words, there was another quake and the ground suddenly settled even lower.

"Go. Now!" Eleanor shouted.

The captain readily gathered the wagon and took to the clogged streets, shouting as he went for everyone to evacuate the city. He and his troops soon came to a place where the fallen façade of a building completely blocked the road. He acted quickly, passing out bags of treasures to his soldiers and sending one rider back with the news. He left behind four guards who stayed in the middle of the street trying to control their horses while guarding the wagon and the city's treasures.

When the captain's messenger reached the princess, she knew it was time to abandon the keep.

One of the outer walls crumbled in front of the departing princess and her troops, and the royal guards had a hard time handling their horses, their eyes filled with such deep fear that they were rolling back in their heads.

They had just passed out of the gatehouse, when another quake rumbled the ground and the buildings around them fell in on themselves and sent white debris billowing out into the street and covering everyone in clinging dust.

The princess and her party made their way back to the wagon. Gwendolyn remained by her side, her bow out and arrow notched. The crowds behind them streamed away from the city and the streets were packed. It was slow going for the princess, but she was glad the warning had gone out and that her people were escaping.

At the wagon only three guards were left. One had been killed by a falling block and Eleanor had to rein in the horses pulling the wagon. She ordered the remaining treasures to be tied to her men's mounts. They then continued their slow advance down the main street toward the north gate of the city.

She kept calling a steady mantra to the people.

"Meet in the highlands. Follow the guards. Evacuate the city."

Struggling along through the refugees, Gwendolyn had fallen slightly behind and was trailing the princess, but in all the terror and pandemonium, Eleanor had forgotten all about her.

The horses could have pushed through the crowds quite easily, but Eleanor kept a slow pace to allowing the people on either side of her to be safe. They all had to urge their horses over fallen debris, but for the moment the quakes seemed to have stopped.

Finally Eleanor reached the north gate. Under the circumstances the guards there were keeping order as well as could be expected. One part of the wall had fallen, and many people were now scrambling over it to escape.

The princess dismounted and ordered her escort to wait for her outside. She climbed the steps to the strongly built gatehouse, and after reaching the top, she stared about in wonder. The sea had flooded the plain. The only opening she could see was one road to the north that was still dry, rising up the incline to the hills.

The city was quickly being cut off. She sighed. At least this side had been built on the highest portion of the hills, she thought. She knew that the dockside of the city had to be flooded completely by now. The water had risen too fast on that side of the city.

A tear streaked from her right eye. How many people there had been too slow to escape?

She quickly climbed down and ordered the Captain of the Guards to stay as long as possible to keep the escapees calm. She mounted up and joined the mass of people exiting the city and soon she was with the palace horsemen again. They all normally could have ridden faster by using the side the road, but that, too, was packed with slow moving refugees.

Gwendolyn had just made it through the gate house and was pushing through the escaping people when the stone of the edifice twisted and great blocks of stone rained down on the escaping citizens below. Another quake hit with a rending, grating sound followed by a gigantic crash behind the fleeing mass.

Eleanor turned and witnessed the gatehouse twist and fall outward, killing many of the evacuees. Others crawled through and over the rubble to gain the road north. She turned and looked far out to what used to be grass lands and she saw that the roads south and east had been swallowed by the rising water.

Still trying to catch up with the princess, Gwendolyn was riding in the rear of the column when more falling debris dealt a sharp blow to her head and she fell from her horse. She landed half on and half off one of the giant stones of the disintegrating gatehouse.

Eleanor kept the masses moving north up the road and away from the encroaching water. Before long she and her troops reached the relative safety of the foothills, but she was still concerned for the refugees of the city.

She stopped on the bald top of a high hill and watched as the people continued making their way towards her. The water was already lapping at the sides of the road and the survivors escaping from the city scrambled to hurry up the incline. Soon the horde of refugees began to thin out and, the last of the escapees, the city guards, marched out of the submerging road, the water up to their knees.

Eleanor went to the guard's captain.

"Were you the last ones out?"

"Nay, my lady," he answered sadly. "Many stayed behind, but as the water rose, we had to leave."

Eleanor's expression was grim and filled with sadness. "I pray then for those souls who stayed behind." She wondered if Gwendolyn had been among them.

Gwendolyn felt water lapping at her feet and sat up, blood covering her face. She wiped the blood way from her eyes and saw water pouring into the street from outside the fallen gatehouse. People continued to try to escape, but the rush of water was too much for them. They quickly turned back to the city to seek higher ground.

Gwendolyn rose to her feet dizzily and retreated to higher ground. The crowd thinned out enough to allow her to break into a run. None too soon, she thought, as another barrage of water began rushing up the street.

She saw a small girl sitting on the side of the road crying, and she scooped her up and swung the child up onto her back. She ran up the street thinking of one thing, getting to the castle. She leapt over fallen debris and shoved her way through the desperate citizens who stood frozen watching the rising water.

She reached the upper levels of the hill that the castle had been built on, but the water still followed her. Gwendolyn passed the wealthiest houses of the city, but their owners had stopped packing their belongings and stood dumfounded, watching what was happening.

"Forget your possessions. Flee for your lives!" a mounted guardsman shouted to them. Some listened, but others could not bear to part with their worldly goods.

Gwendolyn finally reached the castle, but she was not the only one to seek the highest ground. The courtyard was full of people. Pushing her way through the crowd, Gwendolyn continued moving through the castle grounds until she found a stair that led upward to the one standing tower. Most had collapsed in the earlier quakes. The ground shook again, and the tower she was in swayed as she raced up the stairs.

When she reached the top, she looked out upon the disaster that was occurring below. The water had flooded the courtyard of the castle, and the people who could swim sought out the stairs that led up the walls. All about her was water. The sea had reclaimed the land. There was nowhere else to go.

Gwendolyn watched as the walls disappeared around her and the people treaded water in their failing efforts to get higher as the ocean rose. She waited with the little girl in the tower and watched as one citizen after another slowly sank beneath the muddy, debris-filled water slowly covering the once proud city of Partha.

Suddenly the water began pouring into the top of the tower. Grasping the child's hands, she eased her into the water and grabbed a timber floating nearby. There was nothing left to do but swim.

Kicking her feet, she headed north.

CHAPTER TWENTY-FIVE

The elven kingdom stretched from the Mordolwyn Mountains in the east to the Sargorian Mountains in the west and all the way up to the northern sea. It was a vast forest where tens of thousands of elves lived.

The northern ports were some of the most beautiful in all of Muiria. White marble lighthouses could be seen for miles, and the port buildings were made from various colors of marble that intermingled with the tall trees where most of the elves made their homes. Their ships were elegant and sturdy, the bows sporting figureheads of birds in flight, and the elven mariners sailed the seas to bring back materials not readily accessible to their forest kingdom.

The kingdom was equally split up between elves. The High Elves were more magical in nature and preferred cities while the wood elves loved the forest and the wilds, but both intermingled in everyday activities and within the cities. One of the elven clans, though, despite its cultural differences, still shared their forest with their cousins.

It was here in this idyllic setting that the elves had felt the first rumbling of the ground and one tree's trembling foretold the disaster that was to come. When the quakes hit in earnest, the trees all swayed back and forth, tearing apart homes when they uprooted the massive trees of the forest. The elves held on in their homes up in the branches to keep from falling to the forest floor below.

The forest floor started to heave upward and that was followed by a deep drop of the land around. In the north the sea rushed into the ports, submerging them and bringing down trees with its force. The first surge of ocean water destroyed vast areas of the seaside.

The elves who lived by the sea had little chance of survival.

They were not the only ones to suffer. Deeper in the forest the ground gave way, and the sea encroached even further. Many climbed to the highest branches of the trees to escape the flood and others clung to the tree trunks that had been brought down by the force of the water or had been undermined by it.

The elves living closer to the mountains had no idea that the calamity was happening all over the world. They were on higher ground and suffered only the damage caused by falling trees and the occasional collapse of a building from the continuous rolling earthquakes.

As the sea quickly drove inward, thousands of elves were swept away in an instant. The forest floor that rested above the great caverns of the underworld gave way and crashed downward, followed by the ever-increasing depth of ocean water. The quake had destabilized the ground, and the sea was making a great u-shaped gouge out of the forest. Most of the trees had been swamped by the sea. Others stood tall by themselves surrounded by the water.

The elves who had sought shelter in them could do nothing but wait for rescue.

Some elves began creating makeshift rafts with the help of their magic and these flimsy vessels allowed them to stay afloat on the newly created sea. The waters were soon clogged with branches and even whole trees and that made navigating almost impossible without a wizard on board to part the jetsam.

Even so, rescue ships eventually reached the survivors to take their brethren from their perches atop the trees or pluck them out of the water. The elves thought it would take weeks to reach all their stranded kindred, but because of their strong constitution, the elves would survive.

The quakes continued for days. When the worst was over, the elves began to set their lives back in order. Many had died and many more had lost their homes, and the widespread mourning was great in their hearts.

The eastern side of the newly formed sea no longer had any contact with the western side, if indeed anything at all still remained there. Runners were sent to the western lands and they found elves struggling to survive in a small sliver of forest against the Sargorian Mountains. They had lost more of their clans than the east had and most of the western forest was now submerged under water. They asked for aide, but the elves of the east were in no position to send any. They had their own problems to solve.

The subsequent tension between these two clans, those in the west and those in the east, created one of the greatest rifts the elven kingdoms had ever known. It would divide their nation for centuries to come.

CHAPTER TWENTY-SIX

Diordor was one of many nephews to the emperor of Zeiglon and was a captain in the army. He had taken up the fashion of the court and dressed in black, including his mail and helmet.

When the Zeiglon invasion had begun began, his job had been to lead five thousand troops up the coast and close off the escape routes from the city of Partha. It was an easy assignment. The border forts would have already heeded the call to stop the greater incursion into the Parthian northwest. Most all the soldiers would be heading there leaving but a few to man the garrisons of the Parthian border forts.

Diordor was certain he could have his men near the Parthian capital in four days time. Then, all he had to do was wait, but that had been driving him crazy. Finally, the time came and the troops of Zeiglon crossed the border and saw nary a sign of the enemy. Diordor's men quickly surrounded the nearest border fort and talked the Parthians into surrendering. Diordor detached a company to occupy the fort and keep the former occupants under guard.

His command continued on, hugging the sea road, and at each village, the population fled into the surrounding countryside. He ordered that on no account were the people to be followed or was any time to be wasted by his troops on sacking villages.

They had been halfway to their next objective when they felt the first tremble in the ground. Their horses reared and kicked and caused injury to those many who found themselves unexpectedly thrown from their saddles. They righted the column then and began again.

A huge quake hit, not only scaring the horses, but tossing the foot soldiers about as well. Diordor thought at first he was mistaken, but it seemed that the ground in front of him had dropped several paces.

Next he caught sight of a wall of water streaming toward his soldiers from the seaward side of the road. He reasoned that if the ground had submerged, it would only be a matter of time before the water surrounded his troops. He ordered his army to double time up the road.

The water came ever forward and yet another quake hit. This time, he had no doubt that the ground was falling away. He noticed one smaller wall of water heading straight for his command. As the water washed up and over the road, he detected the distinctive smell of salt from the sea.

He called for the soldiers to make their best possible time to the next village. It lay on relatively high ground, but by the time they approached the town, the ocean water was lapping at the roadside behind them.

His horsemen made it to the village first by using a dry roadway, but the foot soldiers who came last slogged through the water while it was lapping up over their ankles.

Another, even larger quake struck. The ground rattled as it dropped lower yet, throwing men and horses about, and small houses in the village in front of them swayed and collapsed.

These villagers had returned to their homes on higher land in order to escape the water, but with the latest quake, a huge wall of seawater bore down across the small town. It began to slow over now the submerged ground, and its waves began to break and strike the eastward side of the village.

Afterward, several huts were washed out by the receding water and then the soldiers noticed that water had surrounded the entire village. There was nothing to be done.

Diordor's command and the villagers alike were surrounded by water. Diordor ordered his men to begin digging soil to create dikes to keep the water at bay as it started to rise again.

Another quake struck, much stronger than any of the earlier ones, and a huge amount of water rushed toward the village, the waves cresting over the half-built dikes and splashing forcefully up one side of the village and down the other.

The villagers and the soldiers were now all in a state of panic, and the horses tried their best to break loose and escape. The water continued to rise.

Before long the village was a foot under water. Groups of soldiers mounted their horses again and tried to make back down the coast road, but they were immediately swept away by the next waves.

Diordor and his command were helpless. Their only option was to wait and hope the water eventually would recede.

The last and strongest quake spelled doom for his command. The water now rushing at them was higher than the tallest building in the village. It struck with such ferocity that men and horses were swept into the deeper sea. Those buildings that still had been standing collapsed and disappeared in the flood waters.

Diordor yelled his last words before the water closed over his head.

"This was supposed to be easy!"

The water crashed down upon him and the weight of his own armor dragged him under the sea.

The first quake had caught Halsbred unaware in his inn. He had been patiently sitting at a table and nursing a goblet of fine red wine while he planned his next step.

His assassins had failed, and Celedant lived. *Incompetents*, he thought, *and my diamonds gone forever*. He fantasized about going after their guild, but that would serve no purpose except to expose him. Besides, Celedant and his companions had ridden with the king past this very window. Zeiglon had crossed the border, and so his job was done. Celedant soon would perish or be captured by Zeiglon's overwhelming army.

It was time to make his way back north. He was sure he had been missed by the wizards of Dragon Isle, but he could explain that away.

Keeping secret the fact that he had turned against them and that he was actually a warlock was going to be another thing, he knew.

His view from the window allowed him to watch as the ground rippled. He saw the building across from him fall in on itself. One end of a beam in the inn crashed down and sent a bed sliding into the common area. He distinctly felt the ground below him drop.

His main self-preservation thought was that he had to get away from the buildings. He was lucky, he silently assured himself,

The wizard ran out the front door just as the second quake followed. The movement of the ground threw him sideways and painfully into a cart, but not painfully enough to keep him from making a dash for a city gate.

He followed the instructions of the city guards and made for the north gate. He had just cleared the gatehouse, joined by hundreds of others, as the third quake struck. He was out on the north road as quick as lightning and he glanced back just as one of the city's outer walls collapsed.

From there he was caught up in the mass evacuation and he headed north with naught but the clothes on his back.

The quakes continued, and he watched as water began to surround the escapees. He surmised that the ground was indeed sinking and he figured that he should head for the foothills. A turn of the clock passed before cheers erupted on the road as Princess Eleanor rode by, encouraging people to make for the wooded hills and reassuring them that the guardsmen were behind them.

"You will be safe in the foothills," she told them and then she herself moved on.

Halsbred was already terribly foot sore, but he thought about striking her down with a spell. He restrained himself.

This disaster was beyond any one person's fault, he thought, and only the gods knew for what whim they had caused this.

It had only been happenstance that Prince Kinemark was near Partha when the first quakes had struck. He and his two thousand lancers were riding for the king's rendezvous point when Partha was evacuated because of the quakes. The sea had risen and there was nothing he could do but follow the evacuees north and offer what protection he could. His sister had the march well under control, he saw, so he held his men back and stopped their advance. He and his troops dropped back as the rear guard.

When they had gone deep into the hills, a scout brought word that a large force of enemy infantry was pushing their way toward the refugees. Kinemark had no choice. They had to fight. He'd rather be out on the open plains of Partha to fight, but he would have to make do with the forested hills.

He watched as the last of the refugees from Partha trudged along, walking at what seemed like a snail's pace beside their laden draft horses and hand pulled carts toward the relative safety of the hills and mountains beyond. As far as he knew, his command of two thousand Parthian Lancers was the last whole unit between the enemy infantry and the fleeing citizens.

After the last of the wagons with refugees and the final walking escapees had all disappeared behind a far hill, he called to his captains.

"Three columns. We'll slow these dogs down. Then withdraw on my signal."

He knew this was far too optimistic because his mounted forces were maneuvering and fighting in a forested land. The enemy would all be on foot and able to move with relative ease.

Before long the sound of his two thousand horses broke the stillness of the trees as they advanced. It took thirty clicks of the clock before the first contact was made when the lead party of the column to his left broke cover into a large clearing.

Battle cries then echoed from the far side, and both forces dashed at each other. In one bone rending crash, Kinemark's horsemen plowed into the foot soldiers.

In the clearing the horsemen had the advantage and they left a trail of dead and wounded behind them, but as they entered the forest again, the enemy foot soldiers that had been held back in reserve rushed in. The Parthians swung their swords downward left and right, cleaving the men rushing about them, and as they died, even more foot soldiers replaced them.

Some riders were pulled from their mounts and swarmed by the enemy, but many of the Parthians dismounted to fight on more equal terms.

All three columns were now in the fight and the companies were pushed forward and backward with the ebb and flow of battle. There was no organization by either side as the two armies intermingled. Both sides sought cover in thickets and behind trees as a barrage of arrows leapt out and took the lives of both Parthian horsemen and Zeiglon foot soldiers.

Most of the Parthians then dismounted and pushed forward into the ocean of Zeiglon's soldiers while soldiers from both sides found themselves trapped and died to the man.

Prince Kinemark, the Parthian commander was killed early in the fight when his horse was wounded and threw him. The Parthian leader broke his neck with a gruesome crunch against the stony ground, but none of his troops knew this, and the battle continued.

As night began to darken the skies, the highest-ranking Parthian captain called the men to retreat. He had been disturbed by Kinemark's disappearance and didn't know what to make of it. Had he deserted?

At the sound of horns from both sides, those still alive from both armies wearily made their way toward the rear. Parthian and Zeiglon soldiers passed within mere paces of each other with nothing more than a nod of their heads.

The Parthians wound their way up to a large hill covered in an outcropping of stone. The exhausted soldiers stumbled along individually or in small groups and for them the worst part of their ordeal was now hearing the wounded Parthian and Zeiglon soldiers in the bloodied forest crying out for help.

The Parthian soldiers could do nothing else until morning. If they strayed into the forest, they would only wander for many turns of the clock, lost in a tangle of undergrowth.

On the other side of the forest, the Zeiglon foot soldiers fared no better. Their numbers had been depleted and all semblance of order in their ranks had vanished. Their commander knew that in the morning he should attack back through the forest, but his command was too diminished for any chance of success.

There would be no true winner in this battle. Both forces had been broken.

With the sea water now beginning to rise around them all, both commanders ordered their soldiers to seek higher ground.

The next morning, the Parthian horsemen who still had horses separated into squads and waded into the chest deep water to search for their wounded, but they discovered many of the wounded had drowned during the night.

CHAPTER TWENTY-SEVEN

Halsbred traveled with the refugees. He felt their hunger and their depression, their sadness of having lost their homes and livelihood. Surprisingly, though, his vision was also of the safety and warmth on Dragon Isle, but his money could not help him in this situation. Instead, he had to rely on his own two feet.

They traveled for days and food was scarce. They stayed along the foothills and watched in amazement as the sea encroached on the lower portion of the land. For as long as the sea's salt water soaked into the soil, the land would remain poisoned and unusable for either crops or herd animals.

The rumors around camp were grim. Everyone knew that they could never return to their land.

While they waited, the remnants of a once proud army found them. Halsbred saw Celedant ride by in brown-stained clothes, and his many wounded were seen to by the clerics who had fled the city. The warlock hated Celedant and he followed and watched the young wizard and his companions pitch a tent and then allow an escaping family to use it.

Halsbred envied the family. If he had a tent, he would never have shared it with these exiles. He did get some enjoyment when he saw the once proud woman of the assassin's guild trudging along on foot in one of her fashionable gowns, now torn and in tatters.

All in all, though, he was miserable.

When all that was left of his army had returned, their march into the mountains began. The cold whipped through his garments, freezing him to the bone, and he tried, but was rebuked when he offered gold for blankets or extra clothes.

He had hated Celedant to begin with, but he now heaped all his own troubles on the back of the young wizard. Now, Halsbred totally despised him.

The march continued, and Halsbred recognized the land around the Stonesplitter clan. Eventually they moved further east and he saw dwarves coming and going on their small mountain horses.

Halsbred remained in the dark about what was going on. He listened to the talk about camp and learned only that they were heading to some land that the dwarves had set aside for the refugees.

Back in Zeiglon, when the ground had first trembled and had begun rising and falling, Zachary, like Aedith, had been burned beyond recognition.

He had tried to crawl to safety, but each movement was excruciatingly painful. The throne had fallen and he had lost his grip of both staffs. His single drive was to get to his inner sanctum to confer with his patron goddess.

Behind the throne a flight of stairs led downward and he crawled to the top of the stairs and tumbled down it, landing with a sickening thud at the bottom of an ill-lit room. His screams, unheard by anyone, echoed off the walls of the small temple.

Across from him stood a life size statue of the goddess, Adois. Even carved in alabaster, her pure beauty shone as a white light beckoning to him. He left a trail of blood from his burned and blackened skin as he crawled slowly across the floor. His skeletal hand reached up and touched the feet of the statue.

Instantly he was transported to a large hall. There, at the end of it, stood his goddess, Adois.

His pain left him, and he looked down at himself to find that he was whole again, his body no longer burned almost beyond recognition.

His goddess beckoned him forward. She looked as seductive as ever.

"So," she began, "you have failed me."

"Nay, my lady. It was not my fault," he replied.

She shook her head. "You had both my staff and my brother's and the power to conquer this world. Yet you failed. You allowed an elf close enough to seize the staff of Adaman...as well as my own staff."

"But, my lady," he tried to explain.

"Enough!" She cried, "You have failed me. Your overblown self-importance has led to your downfall. But I am not done with you yet. I will grant you a boon to live, but not as a human."

"Not as a human? But what...?"

Adois began an enchantment, and pain once more wracked Zackary's body. He rolled on the floor, trying to get away from the white-hot feeling in the pit of his stomach, but the burning sensation only got worse. Zackary screamed and threw up bile as the spell began to work over his whole body. His legs and lower body felt like they were splitting apart as he felt the pain of the transformation.

The emperor's eyes were closed, but he felt his lower body elongating. The pain in his legs was unbearable. He lay upon the floor, the pain still wracking his body, but when it finally eased, he discovered that he could climb upright.

His legs felt odd and he suddenly became aware that he had more than two limbs, but no feet. He looked down and was repulsed. In place of his lower body was a bulbous obscene bloated thorax with eight insect-like legs holding him up. His torso was connected to what used to be his lower body and his skin was rotting and leaking puss out of the burns that had somehow returned to plague him.

Adois laughed.

"You see what happens when someone fails me? You will live forever with this painful reminder of what it means to fail your goddess."

"No!" Zackary cried. "You can't let me linger like this. The pain is incredible."

Adois looked without pity down upon the creature Zackary had become.

"The pain will subside with the passage of time. You may yet prove useful to me at a later period. That will be determined by me. For now, go and suffer in the carcass of what remains of your city."

The emperor felt a dizziness overwhelm him and, in an instant, he was back in the small temple below his shelled throne. Looking around, he screamed and raged over what had become of him.

CHAPTER TWENTY-EIGHT

Two weeks to the day had passed since the refugees from Partha had begun arriving on Stonesplitter land.

The dwarves had given them their own tents and had begun making more, along with providing tarpaulins to shelter the people who had lost their homes. A tent city had been erected at the crossroads leading to Partha and to the Stonesplitter city.

Although the dwarves had offered her lodging in their city, Princess Eleanor insisted that she stay with the people. Prince Kinemark was assumed dead. Those who had survived in the rear guard confirmed that the Prince had not been seen after the battle in the forest. Since then, the people had relied solely on the young princess to rule.

One day several dwarves rode up to Eleanor's campsite.

"The Stonesplitter requests yer appearance," one dwarf said. "He asked that ye please take yer time."

"I'll be along in one turn of the clock," she replied.

The dwarves left and Eleanor began preparing for the meeting. She called together her newly appointed staff and warned them that the dwarves might ask them to move on since food was in short supply. They rode up to the city, the assistants on horses borrowed from the army. One saddle still had brown patches of dried blood on it from some unfortunate soldier.

Gilbert met them on the steps of the old meeting hall. He hailed her with a warmth that a father might give to his children and he even helped her off her horse, although her steed stood taller than the mountain horses the short dwarf was used to.

She stood before him. "It is good to see you, milord."

The dwarf smiled. "Nay, ye can call me Gilbert. It is always good to see ye, Eleanor. I hope this wasna an inconvenience?"

They walked to the steps of the hall and she told him, "Of course not. My people are well off, despite the fact that we have no permanent place to stay yet. But they are staying the course."

The dwarf smiled to himself.

"Well, I may have a solution to that problem. Come take a seat next to me at the head of the table."

They sat and instantly beer and wine were poured for them both as well as for the advisers who had accompanied both parties. Gilbert waited for everyone to taste the drinks before continuing.

"Parchment, please," he said.

A servant placed a sheet before him and he started writing in a quick, nimble hand. He spent so much time on the parchment that the dwarven waiters had refilled everyone's drinks before he put down his pen. He took a huge swallow of beer to clear his throat and turned to Eleanor.

"I must apologize," he said, "but the document is in dwarven. I'm ashamed to say that it's the only language I am able to put in pen to parchment."

She smiled. "I could not begin to script the runes you have so elegantly written."

The Stonesplitter grinned. "What this scribble says is that this is the deed to the Rift Valley to the east. I completely renounce claim to the property and turn the deed over to the people of Partha."

Although she at first had a huge smile on her face, the princess burst into tears uncontrollably and hugged Gilbert. There were wide eyes in the room because that was simply not proper etiquette, but because she might now be the Queen of Partha, the advisors decided that allowances could be made.

The other dwarves were flabbergasted, though not only over that but that their master had just turned over the ownership of the Rift Valley, a place of good hunting for the clan. Gilbert raised his hand to silence the dwarves in the room who were still adjusting to what he had just said.

Gilbert's face turned serious.

"There is one proviso," he announced.

Eleanor's relief suddenly turned to doubt.

"What would that be, Gilbert?" she asked seriously.

A sly smile appeared on Gilbert's face as explained.

"There are always additions to government business like this, but the only one I have added here is that the Partha military will be under my control, should either of us be attacked by an opposing force. Of course, there will be a general to command operations for the Parthians, but they will still be under me control."

The Princess pinched her mouth together and thought for a few seconds.

"That will not be accepted well by my officers, but I see no reason to argue against it. Our people need a new home."

Gilbert slapped her on the back, almost knocking her into the table.

"I will have me scribes who can write yer language draw up a formal document while we dine. Then we can both put our seals on the parchment."

The princess sat back for a moment before speaking.

"I believe that the scribes should call the Rift Valley, New Partha," she announced to the gathering. "That is a name our people will accept."

The next afternoon, when the refugees from Partha had reached the edge of the Rift Valley, their long line of homeless citizens followed a winding road that led downward into the great expanse.

Once there, the army and the dwarves went about building wooden homes to house the refugees. A larger structure was built for the royal family, even though Eleanor knew she might be the only one from it still left. It was rumored that she was using the royal treasury to buy food and winter supplies for all the evacuees, and this "news" made the populace fall even more in love with the young Princess Eleanor.

CHAPTER TWENTY-NINE

Gwendolyn had been kicking her way north on the floating log for two days. She had secured with her quiver strap the youngster she had saved from the fall of Partha. The child had cried most of the first day, but had now finally settled down.

Using the beyond-human strength of her elven heritage, she had kept pushing the log forward. When she thought that she had gone far enough north, she turned and headed toward Partha's shoreline.

She soon came upon a stone church tower and steeple protruding from the sea and she reasoned that the shoreline had totally changed and that many coastal cities had been overwhelmed. Swimming to the tower, she realized she was tired beyond belief. Even her elven strength needed rest from such strenuous and constant swimming.

She settled the little child in one corner of the church tower and draped her wet clothes over her. There was little else she could do for her after being in the water for so long.

The wooden slats that covered the opening of the church tower had survived the flood and were still in place and relatively dry. She broke some off and with flint and steel soon had a fire going on the stone floor of the tower. She and the girl hovered near the fire with their outer clothes now draped on the tower wall to dry. Soon their clothes were dried out by the fire, and the child fell asleep in Gwendolyn's lap, her eyes looking fondly up at her until they closed.

For the first time in days, Gwendolyn was surrounded by peace and quiet. Her thoughts turned to her friends. She concentrated first on the young wizard, Celedant. Her feelings for the human were odd. Gwendolyn had never had anyone but Goran in her life, and she had looked to him as a father. Her feelings toward Celedant were something new. Whatever had prompted her to kiss him was beyond belief. Was this feeling love?

The half elf added more wood to the fire as night closed in upon them. She sighed and tried to get comfortable, but as tired as she was, she felt that her situation was beyond hope. Sleep did not come.

Suddenly she heard a voice call out.

"Hoy, those in the tower. Be you from Partha or Zeiglon?"

To Gwendolyn it was a call from heaven. She stuck her head out of one of the tower openings and saw salvation. A Northman's ship was several yards from the tower and closing. She pointed toward her mouth and began signing. She then reached down and brought forth the child.

The Northman smiled and quickly transferred the two castaways to his ship. They were both given thick woolen skins and soon they were asleep on the deck of the ship.

Hours later Gwendolyn started to stir and a sailor called out.

"Captain, they are waking."

The half elf watched as a portly Northman came down from the steerage deck and squatted next to the girl. He had a ready smile.

"What odd fish to be bringing in. I'm glad we found you or you would not have lasted the night."

Gwendolyn motioned that she could not speak and pantomimed writing on a slab of slate or paper. The captain called for ink and pen and soon she was writing in the tongue of the Northman.

"I am Gwendolyn, the half elf," she wrote. "And I do thank you. I follow Goran the traveler. I cannot speak due to a curse of a Zeiglon warlock. Partha has sunk under the sea. The child and I barely made it out by clinging to a log. She won't speak or tell me her name."

The captain read the note and smiled.

"Well, you are safe now," he said. "Probably the last survivors of Partha. Come, eat, and we'll discuss what happened."

He led her up to his quarters and they ate in silence. It was bland fare because they had been unable to obtain any fresh food at the last port. It tasted wonderful to Gwendolyn, though, and she wolfed down two helpings before the captain could tell her that he could spare no more.

She accepted another piece of parchment and began to write.

"Where are you headed?"

The captain shrugged. "I don't rightly know. At the moment, we're sailing west in hopes of finding land and restocking our food supply. Do you know what happened?"

Gwendolyn wrote furiously.

"Zeiglon invaded Partha, and the army rode out to meet them. I was tasked with guarding the princess. Then the earthquakes came, one after another, and slowly sank the city into the sea. I was following Princess Elizabeth when the gatehouse fell in on me, rendering me unconscious. I awoke later with water lapping at my feet. I saved that young one from a gutter and ran to the castle. The plans were to evacuate and head north to the dwarves. The survivors were to take the north road and head upward into the foothills of the mountains in search of the Stonesplitter clan. It was thought to be safe for the populace. I found a floating beam, tied the child on to it and started swimming north, then east, till I spotted that bell tower."

The captain shook his head.

"Tis an amazing tale you tell. It's a miracle you both survived. With the city gone, and Partha's citizens on the run, there won't be any help coming from them…even if we do find them. We best see to filling our larder the hard way, but my crew are not natural hunters."

The ship sailed for two days, until they spotted land, and they dropped anchor off the coast near a wooded landscape. Gwendolyn went with the hunters after writing down that she was an excellent tracker and marksman with a bow.

On the first day the crew killed several deer and a wild boar, thanks to the half elf's tracking ability. That night they feasted, and the next day they got down to filling their larder and stocking up on fresh water.

The following day she hunted again, but wrote that she had to leave the next morning to search for the Parthians and her friends. The captain gave her a long sword and a bow with two quivers of arrows and smiled as he handed them to her.

"You never know what you might come across on land," he told her.

She surprised him by giving him a hug.

She took up the child and after being rowed to the shore by one of the Northmen crew, began the long walk into the interior.

After several miles the ground turned muddy with signs of the sea's incursion. Before long she was knee deep in the clinging muck. She finally reached a northern road and saw signs of heavy travel. That meant to her that the refuges had reached the safety of the hills.

She turned north in hopes of quickly meeting the rear guard of the Parthians, but it was days before she encountered anyone. Instead of humans, though, it was five dwarves who stepped from their concealed positions.

The half elf mimed that she could not speak and pointed back down the road. The dwarves understood and the elder of the group pointed up the road as he spoke.

"Yer kin are up that away."

A week after they had all arrived in the valley, Halsbred again spotted Celedant. He knew this would be his last chance at dispatching the wizard and thereby saving his own life.

The young wizard rode through the center of the fledgling city at the head of a sizable unit of lancers, all looking like they had been through much battle before traveling north. Halsbred ran alongside the contingent of men following Celedant. Ahead of him the wizard and his companions turned into the royal compound. The lancers made their way past him and headed to a part of town further away where the soldiers were now stationed.

Once they had all ridden past him, Halsbred made his move and approached the main gate, following Celedant. As he approached the guards, he was immediately questioned.

He answered with confidence.

"I am Halsbred of Dragon Isle and friend to Celedant the Wizard. I wish to meet with him."

"Stay here. I will get the court wizard and tell him of your presence," the guard responded.

He returned quickly with his reply. "Celedant is meeting with Princess Eleanor and I bring ill news. It is true that Prince Kinemark has been killed leading the rear guard. I have informed the new castellan of your request, and he will get the message to Celedant as soon as the meeting is concluded. You may rest in the courtyard until then."

A full turn of the clock passed and Halsbred kept near a fire watching the comings and goings of the court staff and listening to the sound of hammering as construction work continued on the buildings.

Celedant appeared at the main door and Halsbred could see the strain that the younger one had been through. He was haggard, travel weary, and he leaned heavily on his staff. Halsbred noticed the bloodied bandage on the wizard's left arm.

"Well met, Celedant," Halsbred called out. "It has been a long while since we last saw each other."

Celedant embraced what he assumed was a friendly, fellow wizard. "Halsbred, I'm surprised you even know of me."

"Well," the warlock began, "you were something of a prodigy, and word of your rise reached all."

"I thank you," Celedant said. "But what brings you here?"

"I was sent to make my way to the court at Zeiglon to test their mood for the masters," the warlock lied, "but as you see, I never made it."

"I have rooms here in the new keep. I can find one for you as well," Celedant assured him. "The princess will be most relieved to have another wizard staying here."

"That would be beyond my wildest of dreams," the warlock replied. "You have no idea what I have endured since the quakes."

"You need not worry any longer, my friend," Celedant said. "Your needs will be taken care of. Go see the castellan and he will find you a place to stay. Though I must say, the accommodations make even our old cells seem comfortable."

Halsbred smiled at him.

"Anything is better then what I have been through."

CHAPTER THIRTY

Over the next two days a westerly wind blew the fog away from the elven forest, showing them yet again destruction beyond belief. Many trees had toppled, snapped like twigs, and the distinctive, foul scent of mud filled the air.

His heart heavy, Treakis began his journey to the Menelwyn capital of Ravannhiel. The paths that led to the interior of the forest were blocked with downed trees and limbs, and he had to dismount and lead his horse past the obstructions. His pace slowed to a crawl.

He neared the capital and he passed workers on the roads clearing the way with axes, and he could again pick up his pace. None of the workers gave Treakis the slightest notice. It was as if the disaster had sucked the spirit from the normally alert, but stoic elves.

When he reached the circle road that went all around the walled city, Treakis saw elves working on the portions of the walls that had been crushed by uprooted trees. Other sections had fallen from the devastating rumbling of the earthquakes.

He approached the gate and saw the king's guards on station, but these elves had clean clothes and freshly shined armor.

Treakis passed the guards with barely a nod and made his way to the king's enclosure. There the city had been cleared of fallen trees and other debris, but beyond there were still massive tree trunks spread out on the ground. Their tops were where families had lived.

Reaching the royal enclosure, Treakis announced his name and a guard hurried away to inform one of the king's aides. Soon a harried looking elf came back to the gate.

"My Lord Treakis, we thought you were lost in the cataclysm...or worse.

"Nay, Witheral," Treakis answered. "I survived where many did not. I have been recuperating with the eastern dwarves after I had broken my leg fleeing Zeiglon." He sighed wearily. "I have important news for the king and queen. May we proceed?"

Witheral bowed. "But of course, my lord. Leave your horse here with the guard, and they will see to it."

The two elves walked in silence. Witheral easily discerned something was wrong and he allowed Treakis to walk in silence beside him. They reached the wooden stairway leading upward to the first huge branch of the tree and they climbed a stair that wound up the bole of the tree into the upper reaches. Finally, they arrived at a great convergence of limbs of giant proportions where a hall had been constructed.

Treakis smiled for the first time in many days. His people were masters of the trees and treated them as gifts from the gods. He felt at home.

Two fully armed sentries let Treakis and Witheral pass, and the two elves proceeded into the interior of the building. Sitting before them were King Roherdiron and Queen Lurie, expectant looks on their faces as they awaited the news of their son.

Treakis bowed and then stood as straight as he could.

"My lord and lady, your son has fallen in battle."

The king looked shaken, and the queen buried her face in her hands and wept.

Finally King Roherdiron broke the silence.

"What happened, Lord Treakis?"

Treakis began the long tale of Aedith's death, of the cataclysmic battle with the king of Zeiglon, and of the breaking of the world as they knew it. He told them where their son's body had been taken and of the waiting for a funeral party to arrive.

"It can be of some solace," the king said, "that our son died killing the despised Zachary of Zeiglon." Roherdiron placed his hand in his wife's. "We must arrange for an honor guard to retrieve our son and return him to his homeland. So many have died, but this death strikes me and my wife as the hardest."

Treakis broke the moment of silence that followed.

"I will guide the party to the dwarven stronghold. Yorgi, the dwarven chief, owes me a great debt and he will accept our company readily. Might I ask," he continued, "did any of my guard return?"

"Nay. None have returned," Witheral answered.

Lord Treakis nodded solemnly.

"It is as I feared. We were pursued by Zeiglon calvary. I hid with my prince's body while the brave guards led the enemy away from us in another direction."

Treakis left the king and queen to mourn their fallen son and went to find lodging and to prepare for his return to Yorgi's enclave.

CHAPTER THIRTY-ONE

Celedant had informed the castellan about the new arrival, and when Halsbred approached, the servant was all smiles. He welcomed the disguised warlock and ushered him to an interior room, no bigger than a closet, with a small cot that took up most of the space.

Halsbred was exhausted and he lay down and began thinking of how he could get back at the younger wizard. Revenge was all that was in his mind and heart as he fell into a deep sleep.

A loud knock at his door startled him and Halsbred sat up straight in bed thinking he had somehow been discovered. It was only a messenger telling him that he had been invited to the princess' table for dinner. Halsbred had slept the day away.

The servant waited on him as he readied himself for the dinner. He quickly smoothed out his clothes and brushed back his wild hair, made so unruly by his harrowing escape. He was shown the way by the messenger and finally entered the finished hall that had been constructed by the dwarves for the princess.

Celedant and his companions sat along with other court notables at a long, rough-hewn table. The princess sat by herself at the head of the table, the usual places for her father and brother left empty except for the banners of Partha draped over the back of their chairs to cover the seats.

The fare was plain, but hot, and tasted like a feast compared to what Halsbred had eaten while on his journey. The older wizard sat across the table from Celedant and his companions, and they enjoyed small talk as they ate the fare.

After their meal the two wizards separated, and Halsbred sought solace in a fine brew the dwarves had supplied him. The others went out to tour the town.

Celedant, Goran and Azimuth walked through the wooden buildings, surprised at what had been so miraculously constructed. There were already houses for many, but the homeless still stayed in tents provided by the dwarves to wait until their new homes had been built.

As they walked, Goran broached a subject none had been willing to discuss.

"Gwendolyn did not make it out of the city," he said, "or she would have found us by now."

"There is still the chance she will walk into camp at any time," Celedant said, still clinging to hope.

Azimuth felt the wizard's deep sense of loss.

"She may still be alive, but we must be prepared for her death. I know you were close with her, Celedant, so rejoice in your memories of her. Do not be overly sad."

If you wish, I can look for her later, Azimuth added to Celedant telepathically.

Thank you, my friend. There's probably not much chance of finding her, but if you think it's worth a try....

I do. And don't forget my dragon sight. I can see in the dark as well as I can in the light.

Celedant looked at Azimuth. He smiled gratefully and nodded slightly. Azimuth could see that the wizard had never had such deep feeling for another as he had for Gwendolyn.

"Celedant, how well do you know Halsbred?" Goran asked to change the subject.

The young wizard shrugged. "Not well. I knew of him, but that's about all."

Azimuth chimed in. *I sense guile whenever he speaks. He is not telling us everything. And I am curious why his dragon isn't nearby.*

Celedant gave him an alarmed look. *Are you sure it's not?*

You know that if another dragon were nearby, I would sense it. I don't. In fact, I sense no dragon presence about him at all. It's as if the two have been separated for a long time.

"Ye don't survive as long as me without being able to judge people," Goran agreed, unaware of the mental conversation going on next to him. "I sense evil emanating from that man."

"Not all who study at Edain can be accounted for once they leave. He is from Zeiglon, by the way."

"That's bad news," Goran said, laughing. "I never met anyone from there that I would play cards with."

"Yes, be careful of that one, my friend," Azimuth added.

Halsbred had had enough time to come up with a plan.

First he would befriend Celedant and later, unsuspected as his enemy, easily strike him down. He thought it would be easy enough to get the wizard to meet with him in the woods outside the new city. There he would attack and kill the upstart.

In the meantime he planned to enjoy the newfound pleasures of the princess's hall.

In the weeks that followed, Halsbred was as jovial a companion as he could be to Celedant and his two friends. He thought that he had gained their trust. Even the dour dwarf Goran seemed to like him and one day Halsbred was invited to accompany the three of them on a trip to the Stonesplitter's city to visit the clan chief Gilbert.

What he did not know was that Azimuth had contacted the elder dragons back on Dragon Isle about Halsbred. The story he had heard and later passed on to Celedant was troubling indeed. None of the other dragons knew about Halsbred's attempts at binding a demon or about what he had done after leaving the Isle, but they knew that his dragon had refused to join him when he left.

They'd heard his dragon had apparently sensed something disturbingly evil about the man and was later bonded to another promising wizard in training.

When the four of them traveled to see Gilbert that afternoon, the clan chief wanted to meet privately with Celedant and the rest of the party. Celedant explained to him then what had happened in Partha, the great rending of the earth and the frantic passage to the north that the remainder of the army had to take. They talked well into the night and imbibed much of Gilbert's fine ale.

Halsbred drank in the kitchen with the chefs and waiters.

That night the clan chief offered them all beds, and the company slept off the ale and broke their fast in the morning with eggs and an assortment of meats. Once finished, the four left to return to the land the Princess Eleanor — soon to be made Queen Eleanor — had named New Partha.

Several weeks later Halsbred found Celedant in the courtyard brushing down his horse one morning. The warlock approached him.

"Celedant, I received a message from Dragon Isle. It is of great urgency and involves you. We must get away from any prying ears and discuss this business."

"Brushing the horse soothes me," the wizard said. "Anyway, I need to exercise my stead. Care to borrow another? We can discuss your letter once we are clear of the city."

"That would be fine," the warlock said with a smile. "I'll follow you."

Celedant obtained a mount for Halsbred and the two men rode through the city and out into the forested countryside. There was a chill in the air, despite it being spring.

They finally reached a clearing to talk and Celedant turned his horse just in time to see Halsbred in the middle of casting a spell.

Celedant threw himself off the horse as a blast of red energy shot through the space he had just occupied. His horse bolted and he hit the ground hard, but he was able to roll away from his attacker.

Halsbred wasted no time in casting another spell that sent small arrows of flame shooting from his fingertips toward Celedant. The wizard felt the flames as he continued to roll along the ground away from Halsbred and one scorching arrow struck him squarely in the back. Searing pain erupted in his shoulder and he came to a stop, his staff held ready, a spell on his lips.

One huge blaze of fire erupted from his staff at Halsbred. The warlock's horse rose up, tossing Halsbred over the back of the saddle, and Celedant used that moment to cast another spell.

Halsbred was instantly ready, and the younger wizard's energy beam bounced off the shield spell he'd hastily erected. The warlock rolled to the side and shouted out a second spell that sent an icy beam directly at Celedant. He saw it coming and danced out of the way, but the icy cold energy put out by the beam threw him several paces back. The beam carried on, struck a tree and covered it completely in ice.

Still lying on the ground, Celedant used his staff to send forceful spheres of energy at Halsbred. Small explosions rained dirt down on the warlock when they landed, making him keep his head low to the ground. One of Celedant's energy bolts hit the tree behind Halsbred, bringing it down with a huge crash and thump, and the limbs crashed down around Halsbred.

The warlock was distracted and Celedant struck again. With a summoning spell he called forth five goblins to attack the warlock and they appeared in a mass in front of Halsbred and started attacking him with their enormous teeth.

Halsbred was forced to draw his sword and fight back by sending spells into them with his staff.

Celedant pulled a healing draught from the inside pocket of his cloak. The wound on his back was still on fire and his left arm had gone numb from the cold ray. With shaking fingers he opened the bottle and downed its contents. Immediately he felt a warm surge of vitality run through his body and the pain in his back and his arm was dulled significantly.

Celedant knew he was no match for the older Halsbred, though, and he drew Dragon Bolt and charged.

The warlock had just killed off the last of the summoned goblins when Celedant reached him, Dragon Bolt at the ready. The sword gleamed red as Celedant struck downward at his opponent and Halsbred was barely able to block the blow and turn away Celedant's attack.

The sword blazed a brighter red, something it only did when evil was around, and the wizard blocked Halberd's lunge and counter-attacked.

Bright red sparks now flew each time the swords of the two wizards met. Halsbred could feel his arm growing tired from the power of each great blow he parried from the young wizard's sword. Celedant feinted low once and then struck high and stabbed deeply into Halsbred's shoulder. He withdrew his sword, now bloodied from Halsbred's deep wound.

The warlock fought on and seemed even more determined now that he was wounded. Celedant was able to block the warlock's next strike with his own staff and the two of them danced around the fallen limbs of the tree as they swung their weapons at each other.

Celedant could barely bend far enough back from the next blow and Halsbred's sword tip ripped through his robe and left a six-inch slice in the wizard's abdomen.

They fought on for many clicks of the clock in complete silence, each concentrating on their sword work.

Halsbred then broke through Celedant's defense and plunged his sword through the young wizard's side. Despite his pain, Celedant was able to react.

Or did he, he wondered.

Celedant could not tell for sure, but he could have sworn that his sword had acted of its own volition.

Then, before Halsbred could pull his own sword free, Dragon Bolt flew at the older man's head, striking across his jaw, ear and skull. The blade was fiery red as the warlock's skull caved in. Halsbred lurched to the right and fell dead.

His body was tangled in the limbs of a fallen tree. His sword was still deep in Celedant's side.

His teeth gritted, Celedant pulled on the hilt of the warlock's sword. He screamed in pain, but the blade slipped free. He tossed it away and then collapsed on the ground.

Swooning in and out of consciousness, he suddenly thought he saw above him the faces of his friends Goran and Azimuth.

CHAPTER THIRTY-TWO

When Celedant woke in his bed, he saw Goran sitting by the door, snoring, while Azimuth paced the floor.

Celedant raised his head and Azimuth shouted at him, "Stay in the bed, for god's sake!"

Goran had been roused and was now sputtering. He knocked over his axe as Azimuth pushed Celedant back down on the bed.

"Lay still," the dragon said. "You have taken a grievous wound in your side."

"All I remember is seeing Halsbred fall…and then your faces, before I passed out," the young wizard recalled.

Goran laughed. "Aye. Young Azimuth here saw you ride away with that craven fellow. By the time he found me, ye had left the city. All was quiet, and it wasna until ye screamed that we found ye. We warned ye not to trust the grimy fellow."

Celedant told the others, "He told me he had an important message from the masters and he needed to talk to me alone. When we reached the clearing, he attacked me. But I'm still alive! That says enough."

"Just barely," Azimuth said seriously.

If it hadn't been full light outside, I would have changed into dragon form and gone after you, Azimuth added. *I'd have roasted that evil warlock before he ever got a chance to hurt you.*

Aloud he said, "Goran, you'll just go on talking till sunrise. Celedant, you fought Halsbred and killed him. He is no longer a threat to you. But you took a bad blow to your side. The clerics have healed it as well as they can. It is tightly wrapped, but you'll be hurting for a couple days. You should be back to normal after that."

"He must have followed us from Dragon Isle," Celedant said to his friends, "and been behind all the troubles we have encountered. I truly owe you two my life,".

"You certainly do," Goran said and grinned, "and I intend to keep reminding ye of that."

"It is time to return to Dragon Isle and report all that has happened here," Azimuth said. "I am sure the masters are nervously awaiting answers."

"Indeed," Celedant agreed. "And yet I fear what the future may bring."

The door to the room opened and standing in the fading sun light was Gwendolyn. She was the worse for wear, her shirt and pants in tatters and her leather armor bearing stains of water and mud.

"Thank the gods I've found you," she signed.

Before she could sign any more, she was wrapped in a bear hug by Goran, his tears rolling unashamedly down his cheeks.

"Me little one," he whispered, "I thought ye were dead."

She, too, was crying. She hugged Azimuth and then dropped to her knees and leaned over and kissed Celedant.

"I thought I would never see you again," she signed to him,

The wizard had no words for what was happening, but the room now seemed to him very small. He tried to sit up, but Gwendolyn's warm hand held him down.

Goran chuckled from the door.

"Yes, yer trapped, me friend. Gwendolyn has taken a liking for ye and she won't be letting go."

About the Author

K.M. Tedrick is a writer and ghostwriter in the fantasy, science fiction, adventure, Christian, and young adult genres with one book that was made into a movie, and over sixteen books published.

Steve Stephenson has written three books in the *War of the Staffs* fantasy series. He has a BA in History from the College of Charleston and an MA in Library Science from the University of South Carolina.

NOTE FROM THE AUTHOR

Word-of-mouth is crucial for any author to succeed. If you enjoyed *The Fall of Partha*, please leave a review online—anywhere you are able. Even if it's just a sentence or two. It would make all the difference and would be very much appreciated.

Thanks!
Steve Stephenson and K.M. Tedrick

We hope you enjoyed reading this title from:

www.blackrosewriting.com

Subscribe to our mailing list – *The Rosevine* – and receive **FREE** books, daily deals, and stay current with news about upcoming releases and our hottest authors.
Scan the QR code below to sign up.

Already a subscriber? Please accept a sincere thank you for being a fan of Black Rose Writing authors.

View other Black Rose Writing titles at
www.blackrosewriting.com/books and use promo code
PRINT to receive a **20% discount** when purchasing.

www.ingramcontent.com/pod-product-compliance
Lightning Source LLC
Chambersburg PA
CBHW010735100726
47899CB00009B/3065